KNOWING JOE

To Margin Joe and Underline Girl,
Whoever you are.

CHERYL ANNE GARDNER

KNOWING JOE

A Twisted Knickers Publication

Chapter 1

Wasn't Aware "that" was on the Menu

I f you were mine, all mine, would you eat pussy with me?" he, my friend Matt, looked over his glasses at me and asked in such a persuasive and nonchalant whisper that my face went hot and sweaty instead of the normal reaction I'd have to his sexual advances like spitting my kale smoothie into his face and/or wetting my pants a little from laughing too hard. I was trying to adjust myself a little smaller between the red vinyl and the grey *Formica* just in case anyone had overheard our conversation when the "What?" came at me as if he didn't already know that he'd embarrassed me to no end. "I don't wear my cape in public; you know that, Girl," and

I did know that, but it wasn't that he didn't wear it in public. He did, except when it was at the drycleaners, which was most of the time. He will never admit it, but Matt is a vigilante and a superhero, standing up for stray cats and feral vaginas everywhere. Or maybe it's stray vaginas? I'm not sure. Back when we were kids, cookie fingers smudging paths along walls fraught with white, I often wanted to pop him in the mouth for the stupid stuff he'd say and the even more asinine stuff he'd do, but then he'd speak to me in this soft, convincing tone of voice — velvety smile to match — and my fists would no longer make any sense to me. Like I said, he's a vigilante, always probing and prodding for that feminist line in the sand.

I like to keep him guessing, though. Mostly because I have no idea what being a feminist actually means other than that I always seem to pay for breakfast, which I did when the waitress came and shoved the check into the center of the table before pursing her lips and sub-sequently stomping off to the disgruntled beard who was screaming for a latté refill at the rear of the establishment. She wasn't coming back, not with a smile, so I drew one on the back of the check then put it and a nice tip under the vase of fake tulips. Matt always says I tip too much, but life is hard enough without worrying about an extra buck or two for a server or the trumpet player illegally busking in front of the tattoo parlor across the street.

BODY PIERCING UPSTAIRS. CASH ONLY.

We don't high tea in the garden district. We don't meander idly through society hill, and we don't stylishly lifestyle atop the row of abattoirs turned art gallery-penthouse apartments near the piers. We live in middle city, the lower digits, between the bodegas, the leather shops, and the homeopathic voodoo alchemists. Where the rubbish only gets picked up on Mondays, and there's no free parking from ten to one, or from two to four, or any time after five. There's an uptown, a downtown, and the equally eclectic and slovenly east and west sides. We are somewhere in between: a six-punch transit-pass away from actual *OZ*. If a city could have a back room, this would be it. Every once in a while someone swaps out the red incandescent for a daylight *led* and cracks the door to let the fart stench out, but it never lasts for very long. The spiritual healing incense and temple gong market only lasted six months. They closed up shop before I had completed my twelve steps to *Zen*, so at this point, I, and just about everyone else I know, well, we have to deal with my roughly sketched out version of normal.

I suppose Matt and I do normal things together. Things people who like each other enough but not enough to get naked on the regular would do on a normal day, in a normal city, with normal lives. We'll have breakfast at a trendy vegan eatery, preferably one that just opened, which means that the health inspection certificate is still live-ink fresh. Not that we are vegan or anything even remotely trendy, but it's nice to have something current to talk about at the cocktail parties we never enjoy going to anyway. Then in the morning, we'll do the dejected servitude walk to our respective work-places, where, we'll blunder away the lucid fragments of the day in an eight-hour stretch of insanity mixed with sphincter-clenching boredom. Matt works in a used bookshop, sleeps on a cot in the mildew-stricken back room, and loves every bit of his sans-the-sunscreen life even though he has nothing of value and wants nothing to replace the valueless nothing he already has. Except me. Apparently, I am irreplaceable. Since the day we met, he's always wanted me as a friend. He's never said that specifically, but I know he does because I'm kind of psychic that way.

"So. How was it for you last night?" he asked of me as we skirted around some dog shit and broken glass on the sidewalk in front of us, and all I could think of was how it wasn't. At. All.

One parking meter, two parking meters, three parking meters, four. We were almost to the bookshop, and I knew my silence was irritating the crap out of him, but I didn't have the nerve to say anything out loud, on the street, in public, where some passer-by might conclude that I was a loser, or worse, that I was afraid, so I flipped him off with a "How was it for you?" knowing full well that he'd gotten himself laid and couldn't wait to tell me about all the transgressive exfoliating and fluid exchanging he'd done upside down on a balcony, or in an alley, or skinny dipping in the park fountain across the street with a watching bevy of tranny hooker mimes. Whatever exotic positioning he had gotten himself into had to be something, anything ... as long as it was daring and social media worthy.

I don't do daring.

"That's your problem," he said. "You have no sense of adventure."

"My adventures are none of your business."

"Girl, a vibrator doesn't count as adventure."

Now, there are six of them in my apartment, and even though I have no idea what they count for, I'm sure that they damn well do count for something.

"So, what was wrong with this one?" he continued, hands deep in the pockets of his drainpipes, keys jingling against his nuts as he snickered and walked. "They all seemed like your type." My type being, in Matt's opinion: buzz-cut bronze with a muscle-stuffed frame, strewn through the sinews with pride and mud. No pulse. No breath. Just a sense of entitlement drooling from the creases at the corners of a pretty, pouty mouth.

Matt and I had gone to a party last night, just as we do every Friday night in the lower digits. Friday is party night. Invitation only. We hate parties. No open air. People stacked on people stacked on people. A suffocating blur of textures, of thoughts, of multi-colored elixirs garnished with opinions *non grata*. I couldn't focus on anything. Just some stranger's mouth, a mouth I thought I might want on mine. Well, for five minutes anyway. Most of the night, I wanted the carpet not to be orange shag and the celery in my Bloody Mary not to be bitter. I often wanted things like that when in the midst of crowd-sourced terror. Matt kept on smiling at me from across the room with an encouraging face full of teeth. I can remember the vein in my wrist throbbing because I had convinced myself that people could probably see my misshapen nipples through my t-shirt. Duncan, Mr. allegedly My Type, and the host, was half-way into a nice beer-buzz, his upper lip sweating spackle into his drink. He talked a good game. Fucked a better one I imagined, but when he nudged my elbow with his, smiled, and then walked his hipster blue-jeans off into the next stupid conversation, all I could think was that he'd look good wrapped in black plastic at the bottom of a ravine.

Five minutes always seems like forever, but that was

all it took to decide that another night of celibacy was a good thing, even if Matt would disagree.

"I couldn't even..." I said as he unlocked and then proceeded to yank the shop door open despite the wood rot and sticking paint.

"Couldn't or wouldn't?" was the question he always asked in return, but this time it was both. Hook-ups don't make any sense to me at all from a logical forward-thinking point of view. I've always got that big-picture thing going on in my head. Instant gratification sticks to my hips in ways evocative of bad science fiction, and just the general idea of it always leaves a scrapyard taste in my mouth. From a practical point of view, I didn't have any condoms, and of late, I've developed a rather nasty allergy to man-buns, elaborate moustaches, *Pabst*, and, hipster cock.

"...and anyway, Matt, you should be thanking me for my couldn't and my wouldn't. Hanging out with Duncan always requires some sort of prophylactic pesticide. I don't know what made you think setting us up was a good idea. Whatcha got in the bag?"

"I wasn't setting you up, and nothing. Just stuff."

"Come on, Matt. Bedbugs? Lice? What sort of creepy crawlies is Duncan infested with now? I don't even know why you hang out with him. Listening to vinyl doesn't make him any less repulsive."

"I like repulsive, and besides, he's got good weed, great porn, and fabulous vinyl."

"Yeah, that's really awesome or something. Now I'm upset that I didn't fall in love last night." I held the door while Matt fumbled through the waft of old paper and WD-40 with his bags of bug spray and his shitty attitude.

"For the love of Pete's piss pot, Girl. You make me insane. You weren't supposed to fall in love last night, you doofus, but you know what I love? I love the smell of WD-40 in the morning."

I just smiled and waved him on through the door.

"After you, bug boy, and maybe you should spray *that* on your crotch from now on; then the bugs will just slide off, and I won't have to shave your fringe again."

Matt just shot me a small crooked smile from the small crooked right side of his scruffy face as we headed into the dinge. The sad thing is that I, too, actually like the smell of WD-40. It smells a heck of a lot better than bug spray, *Lysol,* and shag carpet.

Chapter 2

Tools

M uddled together with the metallic, oily stench of tools, hardware, and lime-scented air freshener, the smell of old paper and burnt coffee hit you as soon as you entered the bookshop. Matt had inherited the shop from his grandparents, and in its former life, long before the city had grown to suffocating proportions around it, it used to be an old-timey style hardware shop, complete with a brass bell on the counter and attentive employees who actually understood what you were trying not to do and what they needed to sell you so that you didn't ruin your entire existence. Matt likes fixing things, and he likes people who fix things, so the old hardware is in storage upstairs for Matt to sell online at his leisure, the industrial steel shelving now filled with books of all shapes and sizes in various stages of moldy decrepitude. Matt bought books whenever he could get boxes of them for a few bucks: garage sales, flea markets, library inventory reductions. Mostly you'd get boxes of paperback romance novels, the kind you buy at the market — cleavage and bare-chested men — but every once in a while, you might find something out of the ordinary. The kind of books book-people collect. Not *cha ching* first editions or anything snobby like that, those were rare finds indeed, and those were for collectors, not real book-people, but sometimes you'd come across old books: illustrated children's books in particular. Books people had loved as a child and had lost during the insufferable press of adulthood. Books they wanted to hand down to their own children or books they wanted to horde for themselves as a security blanket against the monsters that we, as adults, know for certain are under the damn bed. Those are book-people books, and they might command a price of fifty to a hundred bucks if they aren't in bad shape. I suppose that's why Matt decided to endeavor into wordware instead of hardware. Books are the ultimate multi-tool for those who desire to fix things. Meta-physical things. Aesthetic things. Needful things. Most readers don't venture beyond the best-seller list. The people who visit Matt's shop aren't most readers, though. They are anarchists who loathe specifics. They don't care about authors or tropes or top 100 marketing lists. They care about content. They care about art, and they yearn to find something anew as long as it's something interesting, something of an experience, or an idea they've never been presented with before. A well-worn childhood classic often has that effect twenty or thirty years later.

Matt had decided to burn some more coffee, so he'd shuffled off into the back room/hovel he lived in, and I proceeded to shuffle around a couple of newly acquired boxes, Sendak the street cat purring, flicking his tail, and pawing at my feet all the while.

"Did you feed him?" I shouted towards the back of the shop, and Matt yelled back that he had: a bowl of kibble now covered in ants.

"I gave him the bowl this morning, but he was already gnawing on something small and furry, so I guess cereal wasn't on the menu today."

"Guess not. Probably have to worm him again."

"You can do it. He doesn't like when daddy Mattie manhandles him."

"Most pussy doesn't."

"Ha! You don't even know the half of it, Girl. Here's your coffee. I don't have any milk. You OK with slightly charred and some chips off a sugar brick? Ceiling's leaking in the pantry again."

The ceiling was always leaking. Everything was always leaking. Blocked drains. Blocked gutters. Bad plumbing. The plaster and lath just sweat old, damp, and cold all of the time. The brick wall facing the alley never got any sunlight, so over the years it's developed a thick coating of fur inside and out. On a good day, it smells of a green meadow in the dewy-drift of early spring. On a bad day, it smells like a railyard latrine. I like spending Saturdays helping Matt in the shop. The smell of old paper, mildew, and Matt's cologne makes me dizzy in some sweet nostalgic way. It's that soft electrified joy you feel at the anticipation of something new. Something of a secret that's a little bit comforting and a lot frightening all at the same time. A secret that makes you so sweaty that you carry extra deodorant in your backpack so that you can get through the remainder of the day, during which, we'd drink coffee and energy drinks and get Chinese take-away for lunch while we unpacked, catalogued, priced, and put books on shelves sorted by category. If Matt saw something interesting, he'd put it in Matt's TO-READ-BIN under the counter. Matt doesn't own a TV, so when he's not out doing sex, or partying, or hanging out with plague victims like Duncan or boring old loser me, he's usually cuddled up on his cot in the back room, next to the wood stove, reading with Sendak.

Sendak is a very smart and sarcastic cat. I'm sure he's read most of the books in the shop by now.

I opened the nearest box to me. Mostly paperbacks. Cheeky. Lots of man-titty and some dinosaur porn, which Sendak promptly sneezed upon, one book of poetry that smelled like gardenias, which I promptly sneezed upon, and one paperback titled *Men In Love*, which I thought odd because even though my knowledge of men is limited to knowing only Matt and Duncan, I didn't think that romantic love was a consideration for men. Men fall into a lot of things, accidentally, but not love. Not like women do, except maybe in those market romance novels. Holding the book over my head, its drab white cover and yellowed pages breaking the dust-filled sunbeam shining in my eyes, I yelled to Matt, "What the heck is this? Gay romance? Gay porn? What?"

My query was met with a burst of crimson, some

floorboard gazing, and a question mark of its own.
"Who's the author? Nancy Friday? If so, then it goes
in the psychology section. Human sexuality."
"Yeah, OK, but what is it?"
"It's all our dirty little secrets, Girl. Every last one."
I would never tell him I stole the book. My cunning
plan was to read it and then bring it back before he even
noticed it was missing. I turned around and coughed
while bending far enough over so that I could drop the
book into my backpack. I felt like I was MI5 stealing top
government secrets. Sexpionage. I'd write a lady Bond
book about it later and become an international best-seller
and spokesperson for WTF feminism everywhere.
Completely discounting the fact that millions of women
had probably already read the book, I'd convinced myself
in that nano-second that my unique perspective and
insight would be groundbreaking at the very least. At that
moment, I was certain that I'd figure this sex thing out
somehow, come clean with Matt about my affected libido,
and then share my knowledge with women everywhere
at huge public speaking engagements where I would be
presented with a purple vulva of honor for my trials and
tribulations. If they have those. Wait, I'm sure they have
them. They have cock and ball statues for the porn
awards. You can get a trophy statue of anything, I
suppose; although, I've never seen one in a bleached
butthole.

Chapter 3

Crushes don't Mean Shit

M att thinks sexual freedom is some kind of basic right like having long hair, or freedom of speech, or gun ownership. I've read The Constitution, and I don't recall ever seeing a sex amendment in there. I do believe that consenting adults have the right to choose how they express their sexuality — vanilla, kinky, whatever — but what about freedom *from* sexuality? Aren't we allowed that too, if we choose? Or maybe it's not even a choice. I might feel a certain way about things, but my body has its own ideas. Either way, let's face it, sex is a shit-storm. It complicates everything. I can't help feeling that the sexual revolution left a lot of gnarly road-kill in its wake. Now don't get me wrong. I'm not a prude. I don't suffer from a mental disorder either. Lust is natural. Sexual gratification is natural. Sure, I get that. It's healthy to want to do the naked and sweaty *Twister (Ages 18+,)* so conventional wisdom dictates, but hell, feminists can't even figure out what kind of sex isn't some misogynistic plot to overthrow the women's rights movement. Bras and skyscraper heels are the least of our problems.

Sometimes, I think I might want to have lots of sex. Crazy kinky sex. Dirty sex. Soft sex at the bottom of an emotional tar pit. Eventually. Whatever. Maybe not. My body doesn't feel that need, so I just don't think about it. At. All. Not until now. I've never thought sex was necessary. To survive. To Love. All that sweaty hormone-laced crazy gets in the way. Who needs it? I might desire a nice juicy cheeseburger; that would satisfy a pressing need. Starvation is probably shitty, but I don't think I've ever been starving for peen. Not from good-looking strangers or even men I've known and not dated.

You can call me a freak. You can call me a cold fish, a prudish priss — frigid. I've heard all the names before. When I was young, I even believed them for a while. All the other girls talked about boys and what they wanted to do with them back behind the school bleachers. I never wondered about first or second base. That was sports stuff and I didn't do sports stuff, and much like sports, sex was/is a black hole to me, and I am an invisible spinning dot caught in its hormonal centrifuge. Just because I don't get all enthralled when a penis is presented to me doesn't mean I'm passionless though. I've had crushes. Matt and I had crushes on each other for about five minutes when we were kids.

When we were like ten or so...

We'd stolen *The Joy of Sex* from Matt's mother and read it cover to cover in our secret bramble fort in the wooded area behind our houses. Well, we didn't really read it so much. We mostly gawked in awe at the pictures, wondering if we had those parts and how people did that without getting overly tickly. Matt pointed to one of the pictures and declared, right proud, "I've got one of those thingies." Of course, I called him a liar, which resulted in about eight minutes of *am nots* and *are toos*. The only logical kid ending to the scenario was a declaration that we should drop our underpants to prove the what's what.

Matt dropped his shorts first. I remember the plaid fabric hitting the ground in a puff of dust, his shoelaces undone, stretching out from his sneakers like dirt snakes, and the satisfied look on his face as he pointed to his penis and said, "See. Told you." But it didn't look like what was in the book. It looked like a growth or something, so I went over and flicked it. He said, "Ouch," and I said, "Weird."

When it came to my turn, I can remember feeling a little bit queasy. My underpants were white and if they got dirty my Mom would pitch a hissy fit about how I didn't respect nice things when they were given to me and then I'd have to eat liver or something equally awful for dinner because that was shit meat for poor people who didn't treat their things right. From science class, I knew what the liver did inside your body, so it made total sense. Despite the hot metallic taste of liver in my mouth, I pulled my panties down and carefully stepped out of them so they wouldn't touch the ground. Matt lay down between my legs and looked up, disgust on his face, the word, "Gross," on the tip of his tongue. "That's disgusting," he said, "Where do you pee from?"

I just shrugged because I didn't really know. I'd never looked at my vagina from that angle before, let alone while I was peeing. I didn't do that until I was a teenager bent over and perched precariously on the bathroom sink so I could see it in the mirror, and after I did, I completely understood Matt's ten-year-old reaction. It was gross. Alien. Horrifying.

We both pulled our pants up.

"Wanna go to the quarry?"

"OK."

We biked off into the summer heat that day and never spoke of our genitals again, though Matt did let me look at his Dad's porno magazines in an effort to make me feel better about the hot mess between my spindly legs. "See," he said, "They all look gross like that. Hairy yuck," and they most certainly did, so I never gave them another thought, ever, again.

I had only one other crush as a kid.

There was another boy…

It was a summer day. Hotter than small town hell-fire and brimstone, and I was swinging my hips around the inside of a hula-hoop on the sidewalk in front of the local five & dime when I spotted him that first time. I was just standing there all alone swizzling that pink plastic around my tiny waist while the bald-faced hornets swarmed the bottle of soda I had left in the sun to get warm. The boy walked up to me and said "Hi," and I said "Hi" back, cracked my gum, and kept on swizzling. He said he was with the brass band at a school practice earlier. Was still in his uniform. He said it was itchy and tight, and that I looked comfortable in the cheap plastic flip-flops I was wearing. I remember thinking how small my toes were, all tan and dirty, and if anyone might appreciate them as romantic. His mom had got him new shoes for practice. They were shiny, but he said that they made his feet feel hot and cramped. He was on an errand, had to get the laundry at the fluff and fold. He said his mom would be angry if he came back late, wasted his time and her money if the clothes were crinkled up. I told him that he'd better get going then, but he just stood there staring at me. My hula-hoop had ball bearings or something inside of it, and it made this shucking sound as it swung in circles around me. "Would you like some ice cream?" he asked me. I didn't even look at him, just replied, "What kind?" and went on swinging, my tan summer toes gripping the concrete beneath my feet as if the hoop might spin me out into orbit.

"I don't know," he said. "Whatever kind you want, I suppose. We could go down to the marsh, sit in the shade for a bit."

"I don't go with boys," I said all matter of fact like, scrunching up my nose at his boy stink. He said he wasn't a boy. Not in his uniform. That his mom said he looked like a man. He pointed to all his shiny buttons and stuff, so I smiled at him and said, "OK."

I didn't take us long to get there, though it seemed as if it might have been forever, like a time warp paced to the chunky clunking of the heels on his shiny black shoes.

The marsh was a place where teenagers went to smoke and sneak drinks that they stole from their parents' liquor cabinets, but that day we were alone. Just a boy and a girl and the sticky quiet still. I didn't even scream that much when he hit me. It was hot that day. I felt feverish. I don't remember what I'd said to him to make him so angry, and I don't remember much after I'd said it, except my ice cream, melting clotted milk into the mud.

I stopped hula hooping outside of the five & dime after that. I tried to forget what he looked like; his stupid buttons and shoes; that look in his eyes. I would still see him sometimes though, at the back of the schoolyard, lurking in the shadows, watching me write in my diary.

I never wrote about him.

I wrote about what he would never be...

To me.

Chapter 4

Reptilian Brains and Oil Cans

I also met Matt at the schoolyard. He, too, saw me scribbling in the shadows, so one day he just sat down with his chocolate milk container and told me that he liked to go places he wasn't allowed to go. Dark alleys. Unlocked stairwells. The backs of parking lots where they keep the dumpsters, and the basement of his house. He said that he liked to pretend he belonged to this or that other family, that he was the long-lost son of ancient royals, found after years of searching, or that he was the beloved special child who won awards and trophies and would make his make-believe parents proud someday despite his handicap and their stupid. He told me that he didn't like cream of wheat or wearing sandals on the beach because of broken glass or other stuff that could puncture his skin. Said he didn't really like the beach at all. He liked to pretend to make tea in his room for his sister's dolls. She liked it too; though he was convinced his sister wasn't human and that she didn't belong in the family he didn't like very much anyway. His grandma's ashes were on the mantle in a terracotta vessel. He said his mom called it that, but that it looked more like a plain ole jar to him. He said someday he'd break that jar and grind the ashes into the carpet, and that he'd have to do that soon because, any minute, he might change into a reptile with shiny skin and a grand smile and a long tail that had a kink in the tip. "If I were a reptile," he'd said, "Ladies at the market would caress me and say, 'I thought you would be slimy.'" On the way home from the shops, he said he'd break all the eggs in the grocery bag when his mom was yelling and paying attention to the road. I didn't ask about her, but he told me that she was an executive something or another, rode a train, and took power naps when her eyes got weary from looking at him. She drank holy water with rocks in the bottom, and his dad surfed the net, jumping up and screaming whenever someone said something disagreeable. Which was a lot. "Moss is green," he'd said, and for the first time, he looked up and smiled at me as he explained that it grows on his back stoop where the spigot drips on the brick like a blessing. I told him I thought he might become a saint someday maybe, eat caviar and bananas, and wear a bejeweled hat on his head. That he might live in a tree fort lost in the woods somewhere where there weren't any people to tell him what to do. He asked if I would live there with him, and I'd said, "Yes." He said he liked having a plan, but until then, he wanted chicken nuggets and soda and a dime that he could stick in the electrical socket by the boy's bed that wasn't his bed ... just to see what happens.

I barely had to say a word during the entire story, and I think I fell in love with him instantly after hearing it. We've been inseparable ever since. Went to high school and then college together. Moved to the city together. Time has a funny way of screwing with your memories, but if you were to ask me now, I don't think I can recall a time when Matt and I weren't together. Maybe that one time when I had to go into the hospital for surgery to fix my crooked spine and then had to lie in a body cast for what seemed like forever. Even then, he visited me every day to tell me stories about the new bike he'd gotten, or that he'd found gold at the quarry, or that he'd put in a flower garden outside our bramble fort with plants he'd stolen from old-lady bitch-face so that I would have some girl stuff to do when we were hanging out in the woods.

I've never lied to Matt. Ever. I wasn't really stealing the book, but I still felt guilty about it. I felt like I was lying by omission. By appearing, all these years, to be a truly hip sexual being, when inside, I felt like a tin can, which is probably why I could relate to the Tin Man in *The Wizard of Oz*. Well. Sort of. He wanted a heart. I wanted his damn oilcan. When I was a kid, my mom read *Cosmo*, and even today, you can't get through a market checkout line without being bombarded with TOP TEN POSITIONS THAT WILL DRIVE HIM WILD or THE DIRTY THINGS HE LIKES BUT WILL NEVER ASK FOR. Sex is everywhere. Everything is an aphrodisiac and everything will get you laid from body spray to craft beer, and don't even get me started on the dick pills. Natural male enhancements. WTF? I've never understood why people can't simply age gracefully. Why being sexy or being able to get hard is the thing you absolutely cannot lose out of the million other things you can. Penniless and homeless but you can still boink a hole in the wall. Where is the logic in that? Who gave sex that kind of importance over say starving or dying of exposure? And what about bears? I'd rather not get mauled by a bear. Nobody asked me to rank this shit in order of importance. Maybe the answer to it all lay with that ornery little chromosome.

I shoved the book further down into my backpack as I was rustling around for my wallet. I asked Matt if he wanted dumplings or noodles for lunch. He pushed his glasses up on his nose and squinted at me. "Noodles."

He always wanted noodles, and he slurped them up very loudly with those small bamboo tongs you use to get toast out of the toaster sans electrocuting yourself. It worked for him. I've seen him attempt regular chopsticks. Eye-poking type injuries are serious. Your brain is back there, so I never say anything about the bamboo tongs or the slurping. I've known Matt long enough to know that it's best not to question what works for him. Most days he looks like a Mod punk with glasses who recently bitch-slapped a sexy Technicolor cowboy-Jesus and stole his wardrobe. Matt is irreproachable, especially when it comes to noodle eating, his thrift shop/nightmare fashion sense, and his equally disturbing sex life that I've never actually witnessed, thank my lucky stars, God, or whatever omnipotent power presides over that sort thing.

Chapter 5

If Glinda the Good Witch was a Goth named Bitch

W hen I got home that night, my roommate was at work. The bus ride to my downtown apartment was all street-grease, noxious fumes, sweaty paper booze-bags, and novice suits who thought they were above a lowly bus-ride. I was tired, itchy from thinking about Matt's bug spray, and mentally exhausted from all the silent applauding of my future humanitarian efforts. The apartment was dark, except for a muted blue glow coming from the living room and the feeble flickering of the stove light in the kitchen. I hung my backpack on an empty coat hook in the hallway, threw my keys in some indigenous pottery bowl on the counter, put my leftover dumplings in the fridge, and then poured myself a mug of red wine. A big mug. Not indigenous. With ice. Then I stood there in the glow of the streetlights while looking at my reflection through the rain that was nagging at the kitchen window. Tomboy. Twenty-six years old and my own fashion sense certainly hadn't outgrown that designation. A feeble A-minor overture in flannel and raindrops. Maybe our skin is predisposed to certain allergies at birth. I've tried fancy clothes — sexy, frilly things — and heels, but when I try to be feminine like that, like you're expected to be, I just feel like a naked clown on stilts covered in warm soda and hornets. Most women do gorgeous so effortlessly, like RJ with her creamy mocha-latté skin, the light dusting of freckles on her cheeks, and the hint of tangerine in her afro when the sun hits it just right. She's pure poetry inside and out and she never needs to fake it. I do. Fake it. If there's poetry in me, it's underneath all the chipped paint and graffiti. Speaking of RJ, there was a note stuck to the fridge from her addressed to me:

UR TURN TO GET WINE, GIRL.
RED
NOT SHIT
&
RAMEN

My roommate, Rita Janine, is a geriatric nurse. She works the nightshift mostly at one of those care facilities for dementia patients, so in this reality, we exist on two different inter-dimensional planes, overlapping, but rarely connecting except for the particles of dust small enough to penetrate the barriers in the gravitational space between the planes. Translated: *post-it* notes on the fridge, text messages, and status updates to social media sites. Her long-time partner, Bitch, is a Goth-punk tattoo and piercing enthusiast or something equally dark and sparkly and twisted as long as whatever it is involves black nail polish and combat boots and a whole lot of art-house horror films where the blonde chick doesn't die as soon as her tits appear on screen. I like those too. Maybe I'm Goth and just never figured out the eye makeup or found leather pants that fit me right. Leather is difficult to pull off, figuratively and literally. I'm pretty sure only vampires can do it with any grace.

As I was sipping my wine, I heard the flick, flick, flick of a lighter, then a faint bubbling, followed by a slow exhale and a softly whispered expletive.

Even though I'm not hip or trendy, I like Bitch. She is a true artist, and so the apartment is littered with her art deco stylings and huge vagina sculptures in a variety of mediums from paper mâché to sandstone. The bigger the vag is, the grosser it looks. Bitch calls them gashes — the metaphoric wound that is woman — symbolizing our suffering at the hands of the patriarch. I don't like that word — gash — but I sort of like the art. I can take all the folded grossness, the red paint, and the militant feminism, but if she starts putting murkins on the sculptures, I'm moving out. The screaming sex-addict douche-nozzle in the apartment above us, the one who sounds like he's bowling with his testicles from one to four AM, is enough uncomfortable for me outside of pantyhose.

I grabbed my backpack off the hook and walked into the void of kitsch I call the living room, even though I wouldn't say we actually *live* in the room: we exist in the space sort of how lichen exists on a rotting tree stump. Bitch was getting high and watching her favorite film: *I Spit on Your Grave*. Not the remake. I threw the backpack on the floor next to the tatty second-hand seventies nightmare I call a sofa, sat down with my wine mug, and kicked my shoes off.

"You need more wine," was the hello I got upon sitting down, and since I knew that we did and that a sunken living room to match our sofa would be better, I just nodded my head and started unpacking my backpack. "I need some more paint, so if you want, I can go with you to the shops. You want a hit off this, Girl?"

She offered the bong to me, but I really didn't feel like getting high. "Thanks, Bitch, but no. Not in the mood today." I looked over at the TV. "Did the chick cut off that dude's pecker yet?" It was my favorite part of the film, and Bitch knew it, so she just laughed, told me I'd missed it, and asked me if I wanted her to rewind.

Bitch loves people, not all people, just certain people, and it doesn't matter if they are men or women. Some would try to slap a label on her, but she would just say, "Fuck all the way off," that she isn't anything, that she won't be boxed in by expectations. She says that her idea of love has nothing to do with sexuality at all. "Love is a companionship and compatibility thing," she often says, "It's about compassion, trust, and understanding. It's about being with someone who gets you and is willing to go along for the ride," and while Bitch might look like a wild ride with her chalky black hair, tattoos, piercings, and platform shoes, she's one of the gentlest militant feminists I know. Maybe it's the way she looks at Rita

Janine. It's almost as if she gets lost in the idea of her, like RJ is the most special, honest, original thing on the planet, and it makes my heart sink a little bit. Envy? Maybe. Especially about the original part. I don't really know where I fit in the human world. Plain Jane Jones. Or maybe it's Jane Doe. I'm just a girl who doesn't even know what girl means let alone how to be one. It reminded me then of those stupid *Playboy* magazines. Bitch was sucking back another hit when I blurted out, "Is that what a woman is?" and since Bitch had no context with which to answer the random internal thought I had foisted upon her mellow, she just looked at me like I had no eyebrows. She thought I was talking about the movie when she replied, "Shit yeah! Smart, strong, righteously angry woman getting revenge. Yes. Hell yes!"

I didn't really want to correct her since she was in the zone, so I grabbed the bong from her, took a deep hit, and whispered a barely audible and smoke-filled, "*Playboy*," to which she replied, "What about it?"

After about five minutes, the room I exhaled into felt a little softer, the TV a little more distant. I hadn't responded to the "what about it?" question yet, but in the smog-filled serenity of my tacky living room, I felt comfortable in the moment to go there with Bitch.

"The *Playboy* models, is that what men want?"

"You mean the airbrushing and the perfectness? The likes horseback riding, reading gothic poetry, and the working on the biochemistry degree bullshit?"

"Yeah, mostly the perfect part. Those wide white smiles and the perfect plastic *Barbie* skin bathed in angel-halo light. Is that satisfying, you think?"

"It's a fantasy, Girl. Everyone needs fantasy from time to time, so, of course it's satisfying in that small moment when it's needed. When *they* are in the throes of desperation with their hands down their pants and there's no one else around."

"Like cannibalism?"

"What?"

"You know. You're starving. There's nothing to eat but maybe the neighbor you can't stand, and there's no one else around, so you're only thinking about how hungry you are, and things start to get a little bit sweaty, Manilow is playing in vinyl, and they, the neighbor, are naked all of a sudden, looking all basted and juicy in hipster socks and sandals, and you can't help it, *but*, you'd never do that, *but*, you're hungry, hungry, hungry, and that man-bun is the most absurd hairstyle you've ever seen outside of a mullet, so you want to grab him by it and twist his head off like a roasted turkey leg at the Renaissance Fair. The next thing you know, you're a salivating mongrel dog cutting your bicuspids on a hairy shin bone."

Bitch just looked at me, google-eyed, mouth open. She had to take another hit before she could even speak coherently, before she could say, "Wow. For someone who doesn't date, barely even talks to men, and never has sex, you sure know exactly what it's all about, Girl."

Now this statement shocked me, and I began to wonder about that collective subconscious thing and the fact that maybe, probably, I had inherited some rare insight. Something had happened while I was in the womb. That's it. Too much mosquito fogger and the nitrate in the hot dogs and pickles my mom ate while I was in utero. Maybe I should have been a dude, and all those puerile and unmentionable musings cluttering my think-hole were inherited from those prehistoric beings I normally considered strung out on sex and dirty in a not very hygienic ball-scratching way. I have thought about eating my neighbor on occasion, so maybe I did have a handle on this male fantasy thing. I thought about that for a minute. Then I thought about *Playgirl*. Didn't that magazine only have like three thousand subscribers? It has relevant articles. Nudie dudes too. Are women embarrassed about naked desire? I mean, women have fantasies too, right? Women get hungry too. I've over-heard enough bar and office conversation to know that women get thirsty. *Yeah. I get it.* My stoner confidence was kicking in. This fantasy thing isn't all that complicated, or so I thought, until I opened *the book* and realized how wrong I actually was.

Bitch was so stoned that she finally couldn't resist the urge to sleep, and, since my mind had been cast into turmoil at the taste of hairy shinbone in my mouth, I couldn't sleep, so I decided to start reading the book I had so stealthily pilfered.

I wasn't even five pages in before the underlining started, and I *was not* emotionally nor academically prepared for the sort of enlightenment I was going to find in those musty pages. Certainly not while I was stoned. There were entire passages underlined quite vigorously, passages that contained the words Love, and Rage, and Victim. Even Humiliation and the word Forbidden were often melodramatically attached to the word Pleasure.

I felt like a third-grader trying to figure out build-your-own furniture instructions. My best guess as to what the entire mess really boiled down to was that, to men:

WOMAN = INHIBITION, RESTRAINT, AND GUILT.

So, in extrapolating an answer from that equation using the primitive algorithms I had at my disposal, I concluded that when men treat women with love, affectionate understanding, and compassion, they are embracing the idea that a woman is a cold-blooded and callous screw at the local lockup. Conversely, when men treat women like dirt on their shoe, it's an obvious revolt against feminist control. Seems women aren't the winners in either scenario.

Underline Girl was angry, and that made me angry.

I thought of my mother and those white panties.

I thought of my ice cream sliding into the mud.

I thought of those *Playboy* models and the acreages of expertly sculpted vaginal shrubbery, and I, too, felt the rage.

All the way down to my liver.

Chapter 6

Joe

J oe cheats. Underline Girl says he thinks he's too dirty for her. *"Joe does this. He denies me my sexuality."* She seems angry and hurt, the way she digs the ink into the margins. I wish I could talk to her, but not because I have any insight or anything of value to impart to a conversation about a personal betrayal like that; it's just that I'm an introvert and I'd rather listen than speak. Inner conflict interests me in a contact-high sort of way, and on the opposite end, having someone's undivided attention upon which to unload your misery is addictive for most non-PhD in psychology people. It's a negative energy transfer, like confession, and they feel relieved when it's over I suppose, but Underline Girl seems more lost than angry because all she has is her own biased interpretation of the words on a page. *"I wish that were the case with Joe; his orgasm is more important than mine."*

Do I project my fears like that? Is what's between a woman legs an extension of her inner self? What's so important about it? That hole. That orifice. Does it define her? Is it loveable, desirable? Does it really need to be waxed and steamed?

Does sex make a relationship?

Does sex make men cheat?

Is orgasm some sort of prize? And if so, who wins?

"I wish Joe would get off his stubborn ass and be a real lover to me. I hate his attitude."

Women always get the blame no matter what despicable and vile horseshit their men get up to when they think no one is watching. *"This is Joe; I hate him for cutting me off sexually."* Society says, "We can forgive a few peccadilloes." It's always the wives' and/or the girl-friends' fault because women are manipulators of demonic proportions, single-handedly orchestrating all of the male madness in the world. Joe would never cheat on me. Would he? Maybe Underline Girl just didn't get the kind of relationship he wanted. Maybe it was only a friends with benefits sans option B. Wait. That's judgey. See, I'm blaming her now for not getting it. Why don't men have to pay attention? I wonder what kind of relationship Joe really wants. If he wants a relationship at all. What kind of sex does he assume Underline Girl can't give him? Does he want the overly dramatic tie-me-up tie-me-down girl where every day is a carnival ride of face-sucking contemplation while each is silently plotting to light each other's pubic hair on fire? Literally.

No. Not good. That doesn't seem like a Joe thing.

"Joe's attitude is this to me: infantile and angry."

Maybe he wants the obsessively over-focused on his dick and only his dick, "I worship you," type girl. The girl who's worked out elaborate sketches, illustrating how the two of them could be conjoined by some internet Body-Mod doctor in Slovakia. A co-dependence girl. Can't live without him and keeps his dick pics and toenail clippings in a box next to the bed for future voodoo rights.

Ugh. That's scary.

Social Butterflies seem nice, but it probably gets tiresome having to find places to do coitus at all the parties and social functions. Other people's beds. Coat checks. Public toilets. No alone time ever and public toilet seats. Please ladies, stop peeing on the toilet seats. You are worse than men, seriously, but I digress...

Maybe Joe wants a hate/hate hook-up?

No. That always ends with jail time.

Joe and Underline Girl seem like hot, spicy fighters. I guess all the slapping and name-calling and degradation is foreplay of a sort. I've heard that makeup sex is the most awesome kind of sex, but then again, the people who've said that to me always seemed either angry or were crying when they'd said it.

What kind of relationship do I want? Might Joe be the kind of guy who wants to marry you after the first date? Kismet Guy. That first kiss soulmate Disney movie legend load of crap.

Dreck, right?

I don't know if I buy into the soulmate thing. I've seen it happen, and then I've seen the divorce happen just as quickly. Someone comes home late, later, the next day. Underwear is missing. Lipstick where it shouldn't be. That faint smell of someone else closer than might be construed as appropriate in polite society. That hot musty stench that penetrates your intestinal tract like a steel-toed cowboy boot so that you're plopping rusty spurs out of your ass for three weeks before you decide to hack their mobile.

Was he flirting with the waitress?

Or the waiter?

You'll have to ask his funny-guy best friend. Sexy, smart Kevin. Kevin will let you sob on his shoulders. Kevin will tell you the truth. Kevin will smile and tell you that you're his friend too while he tries to get two fingers up in your crotch.

Fucking Kevin.

Oh God, what if Joe prefers bromance and superheros to horror movies?

What if he has phobias about attics and basements and hardware shops? If so, I don't think we'll make it. Is that something to ask on the first date? Before or after he proposes to me? But what if he's into horror movies too much and his family is a bunch of inbred psychotic clown cannibals? Though, if he wanted to watch sentimental rom-coms all the time, I'd have more trouble with that. One woman on her period in a relationship is more than enough. That's a stereotype, too. I'm scared. What if I'm not ready to be in a stereotype with Joe? I mean, I'm good at being me. Just me. I enjoy it. Other than Matt, I don't get attached easily. I'm not very sentimental, I guess. I don't save birthday cards, and I don't wax nostalgic over elaborately crafted scrapbooks. Being a hard-ass is my default setting. Maybe I'm afraid of the "didn't work out in the end" thing. That won't happen to Joe and me. Will it? No. We'll fall in love fiercely. No regrets deeply. Everyone will be shocked. Everyone will have his or her doubts. "It'll fizzle out," they'll say. Matt will ask if I like Joe or do I "like like" him, with air-quotes. Will I know? Will it be real or will it be trying too hard? Will I be letting myself get taken advantage of? By a cheater. I'd been warned. By Underline Girl. She wore her heart on her sleeve. Pink-tinged with denial all to save some pitiful soul like me. "He'll come around," I'll say, just like she probably said to herself a hundred times. A thousand times through tears and cheap wine and schmaltzy music. Dub it out girl, because he won't.

He won't be coming or going around anything.

What do I know though? I have no experience in dealing with any of this. I never went to a single formal in high school. It was Social Science, but there wasn't a test, so I skipped it. I skipped everything that might have given me feels or cooties. I've never fallen in love or had crushes, other than those five minutes with Matt. School-boys always wanted to rush into it. Intimacy doesn't mean naked. It's too much pressure and way too much immediacy. Would I have to say no to Joe when he puts his hand up my shirt? Explicit consent. I've never given that — ever. Joe will understand. He won't be crude. Won't say, "I wanna bang you." He'll wait for me to kiss him back.

He'll be careful.

I won't be.

I'll get caught up in the moment. Shit will get serious, and I'll say the L-word too soon. I'll blurt it out after only a week of the every-waking-minute crap we tell ourselves is more than just scab picking. Then the entire thing will skid, tits first, through a river of cherry-flavored lube into a black pit of abysmal failure. Doesn't it always?

He will tell his friends that he banged it, hit it, crushed it, and mangled it ... I probably won't even come.

Things will be awkward from that moment on. We'll go on a break. What is a break, anyway, if it's not something that accidentally happens to your femur? Who defines this shit? Just because it doesn't have the word UP after it makes it something different.

Is it false hope?

Yes.

He'll cheat.

He'll find some real girl who can wear stilettoes.

Who has the upper hand here?

I'll cheat as a cop-out, and Underline Girl and I will meet for margaritas every Wednesday so we can cry, lick salt, and become terribly bloated and undateable.

Matt will buy me bug spray.

That's what Matt does.

Chapter 7

Clubbing Sucks ... It Just does.

O n Tuesday nights, we often go shoe-gazing in an old converted warehouse at the intersection of 5th and the train tracks called *Club Grind*. It's fondly known around the lower east side as a Unitarian Universalist club because all are welcome, including the 'just trying to figure it all out.' I let a woman seduce me there once. Sometimes my curiosity gets the better of me. There was something about the way she moved across the dance floor, all quicksilver in crimson, nipples pressed hot and tight against silky fabric. I'd had a few too many drinks, and Matt was nowhere to be found. Without him to restrain me, things often plummet into chaos right quick. She, the woman who seduced me, was flirting with the bartender, not me, so I told her I liked the way her skin looked against the lights and colored glass. Innocent. Sparkling. Like she was dusted in the 70s. She wasn't a she though. She was something like me, but more dangerous, more exhilarating. She held out her arm. There was barely any flesh on it. Tattooed Bone. Black Market Ivory. The way she looked at me, kissed me in the alley after we finished a smoke.

My Luciana.

That's probably the only fond memory I have of the club scene aside from the music.

I'm Matt's wing-chick, you see. I know. It's supposed to be wingman, but Matt explained that, "Men wings are all a big bag of suck." He never explicitly said that I was his wing. I'd always just assumed as much because Duncan's an idiot and the biggest bag of roach-infested suck you've ever seen. It's better than a bag of dicks, but only slightly. When you start pulling things out of the suck bag, you start to understand the complicated yet subtle nuances of the situation. Wing*men* can't be trusted.

1. If they find your target's friend less than desirable, they will throw you under a bus by ditching you the first opportunity they get. This might happen with or without an excuse. If there is an excuse, it's usually lame like accidentally leaving the gas on or a plumbing issue at their apartment that is somehow rescue dog related.

2. They will hit on your target the first opportunity they get, if they think she's hot enough. The usurping in

this instance does not require any justification. They'll use tactics like buying her extra loaded drinks or complimenting her lime-green toenail polish and ankle tattoo.

3. They will either humiliate or embarrass you in front of said target by insinuating that you are creepy or sexist ... or both. This is done in order to make their own damn selves look like a better option than you do in order to facilitate the usurping outlined in item number 2, sans the drinks and tattoo, toenail noticing thereof; though gas lighting is always an option should resistance be encountered.

4. Duncan. Mostly because of the *Pabst*, which is gross.

Being wing is something of a bro civic duty, and serving as such is how I wound up with more than half of my social media friends, including Luciana. A night of clubbing with Matt always meant that I'd have to find my own way. Tonight was no different...

The smoke machine was billowing at full force, and the club was a mustard-slathered tin of sweaty, oily people in their twenties and early thirties, all dressed in varying degrees of hipster second-hand-wear. The music was not horrible, but the vintage disco lighting was giving all of the people on the dance floor seizures, or something that resembled such: faces twisted, sweaty flyaway hair, drinks in fancy glassware being swished about in the air with little respect for the who, what, and where upon which it would be splashed. It was all better than my dancing though, which Matt endearingly called the spastic chicken. I blame the scoliosis in my childhood for my rather slant view on public dancing as performance art. I spent most of the evening darting through fast legs and flailing arms in search of Matt and Duncan, but I couldn't find them anywhere — again. Obviously, they'd bagged their quarry early and were off somewhere, naked, sorting out the spoils. I had to tell myself, "Do not try to picture that. It will only give you nightmares," so I blocked out the grungy nudefest coagulating in my liquored-up noggin, and I continued my attempt to conquer the gauntlet, until finally, I reached the bar, and it was so crowded that I had to squeeze between two hulky leather-queens to get anywhere my feeble money-waiving hand might garner notice from the bartender. One of the leather-queens looked down at me through lashes so long you could use them for boating the clouds on your way to the Kansas poppy fields. I leaned forward, craned my neck a bit, and looked in the other direction in order to discourage conversation, but before I knew it, her hairy arm was reaching for mine...

"Cadavers," she said to the leather-clad mountain next to her in a gruff old-lady smoker rasp. The other turned to reply with a, "Totally predictable. Emaciated. Tweeks and Twinkies," and I was stuck between them and their snarky banter, a hairy, peck-stuffed, and bedazzled brassiere pressing into my face hard enough for me to smell the *Old Spice* in her tit-hair. I thought I was going to lose consciousness, but at the onset of total cologne asphyxiation, one of them spoke to me, "So what do you think, hon? Is there anything even remotely fuckable in this joint tonight?" as if I would know, being an actual expert and all that. "Even lickable will do," said the other one, who was starting to look like a skyscraper with all the flashing disco lights reflecting off the black latex she was wearing. Her updo did sort of look like gorilla pubes, but I thought it best to keep that to myself, so after scrabbling for some air, I said, "Ladies. I kinda have a thing about heights, and I'm really, really thirsty, so can one of you grab the nip-rings on the beefy bartender. I'm buying. Then we can sit down and assess the room before we sweat each other up down to our panties?" They both just laughed and then said, in unison, "We aren't wearing panties." All I could think about at that moment was Matt's bug spray.

Once we got the drinks all sorted out, we managed to find a large round table in the balcony overlooking the dance floor. Because of some mathematically complicated engineering principle I don't understand, the acoustics in the place kept the music bouncing around the bobbing heads below us thus allowing for conversation at a decibel level that didn't require screaming at each other. This was a blessing because my voice was already hoarse from the cloud of fake chemical smoke we'd been gasping about in all night.

Despite my throat feeling coated in sandpaper, I was enjoying myself. Apparently, leather and flannel go well together, so well that our table became the tantalizing center of attention, drawing the type of crowd normally reserved for X dealers, porn peddlers, or drag performers who looked like celebrities. In assessing the crowd, we all came to the same conclusion: as far as finding anything fuckable here, the place rated about the same as a 14th Century taproom during the height of the bubonic plague, so the conversation moved to baristas and coworkers. I warned my newfound friends not to get me started on men at the office, because most of them are about as useless as a bag of rubber dicks.

Life contains a lot of bags of things I've discovered, but the businessman douche-bag, they are special with their prancing around in their perfect suits and their speaking about their perfect stock portfolios and their perfect downtown apartments with UV filtering floor to ceiling windows that overlook the city from such and such an angle and distance that all the unsavoriness of actual city life is rendered inconsequential. That's the point of being a rich hipster, I guess: keep your fancy pants ego so far up in the clouds that you can't see the shit on your shoes.

Most days I just slouch down in my cubicle trying to blend in with the mazy sea of grey walls, grey carpeting, and framed inspirational art. Making yourself invisible is skillage a level above meth making and light wizardry. When it didn't work, I'd spend those eight hours listening to inane what I did on the weekend stories, my kids are so awesome stories, and/or when and where I no-condom-banged some sociopathic stranger while I was blind puking drunk stories. The highlight of the workday being the lunch order. Nevertheless, even all that was better than spending eight hours with my boss's greasy meat paws on my shoulders as he perused reports for imaginary errors in order to give him an excuse to stand close and grind his stench-crotch into the back of my chair. Repugnant was always the word that came to mind. I'd have to ride the bus home smelling as if I'd bathed in his dollar-shop body spray. It was all so depressing that I'd spend my goof-off time writing on the greasy lunch menus that would somehow always wind up on my desk even though I never ordered lunch. I suck at poetry, so I stuck to Haikus about the dismembering and the subsequent cremation of executive bodies. I'm sure burning *Brioni* smells better than the lunch orders.

I did have a work-a-day sanctuary though, and for a time, it used to be private. I'd sneak away a couple of times a day to catch a smoke amidst the bleach and other toxic chemicals in the janitor's closet on the customer service floor. In customer service, nobody gives a shit about anything. If you want to microwave popcorn in the nude with your hair on fire while drinking a martini, nobody, not even the supervisors will notice. The only thing they'll ever notice is if you wear jeans on a non-jeans day.

Sid, one of the other number jockeys, started joining me for a smoke about a month ago. He's a little creepy but harmless, I think. He likes to stare at my legs with his squinty blue eyes, and I caught him stealing the Haikus from my trash bin a couple of times. Other than the fact that he likes bad poetry, ugly ties, and the smell of bleach mixed with menthol cigarette smoke, I don't know much about him. He never says a word to me. He might have some sort of lint fetish too because he spends an inordinate amount of time picking it off his clothes and putting it in a little mason jar he keeps in the second drawer of his desk. I keep meaning to ask him about it but haven't found the right words to approach him or the subject. I get the impression with Sid that the right words are important. Otherwise, why say anything at all? Which is why I think dating should be a silent endeavor. Maybe flash cards and a quiz would suffice. Weed out the potato heads first, and then you can work on the racist redneck homophobes and the muscle-bound uber-putzes who clearly don't know how ladies operate on an academic level. In college, Matt always questioned my resistance to dating and random sexual encounters, but really, come on, half the time I felt like I was trying to teach language skills to retarded amoebas and failing so miserably that I couldn't even, to which Matt would always reply with something along the lines of: "Stop it, Girl, you are being so melodramatic and cliché." I probably was, but here's the thing about clichés: when a thing becomes so prevalent and trite that it's a joke, it becomes a cliché. I haven't met a single man, other than Sid, who wasn't a cliché poster-boy, and therein lies my dating dilemma.

Sometimes I run into Sid at the clubs. He's a good dancer. Drinks martinis with three olives and a lemon twist, and still can't force himself to speak to me. I saw him on the dance floor a couple of minutes ago, waived him over to our table, figured maybe with all the extra drunk and jovial people around he might feel comfortable enough to articulate something, anything at all, but in a moment of distraction, I lost him in the undulating crowd. He, too, disappeared, just like Matt and Duncan.

The entire night wasn't a total loss though. Despite all the hard lines, the greasy abdominal muscles, and the fierce updos, it turns out the leather-queens were both investment bankers, and after about twenty or so rounds of tequila, I learned how to grow herbs on my balcony and my retirement fund was secure.

Chapter 8

Sometimes, Luxury is What You Need

I decided not to go straight home from the club. I decided to see a peep show at a theatre down in the art district after my new drunk-assed, leather-clad acquaintances said that they weren't ready to embrace the sunny side of life yet. Their real world seemed about as painful as mine was, so I offered a suggestion, that, outside of energy drinks and cattle prods, just might keep them purposefully breathing for another hour or so.

My friend Sebastian a.k.a. *La Fonda Ian Dark* worked the smudgy glass down at Larry's Lush Interiors (Larry Luxe for short) three nights a week when he wasn't busing tables and washing dishes at my favorite diner.

He and Bitch went to Art College together, or got tattoos at the same place, or maybe it was that they met at the co-op over sexually explicit fruit or something. He was a ballet dancer. Some theatre. No prospects and rent to pay, like so many other artists we know. After I see one of his shows though, I am always left speechless and amazed at the fact that he is not famous.

He can work the glass like nobody's business. When he becomes La Fonda, his entire persona transmutes into sticky chocolate caramel laced with bourbon and meth. She looked so edible divine on the other side of the glass. So hot, bent over, the length of her hair spilling onto the shabby lacquered floor, the dragon tattoo on her ass lashing its tongue around her buttocks, gently licking at that place no man was allowed to go.

Everyone wanted that dragon. Every pathetic, sad, and lonely person, and every pervie wanker wanted to feel that dragon's breath in flame and in ash. Even my slack-jawed leather enthusiast friends suggested to each other that there might be room for a third at their fancy condo, but Sebastian was in it for the performance art of it. He didn't dabble in back alley grease.

La Fonda did several pirouettes then turned around and sat down in her souped-up dentist's chair, her skin slick against the white leather and chrome. The patrons in their little booths would cheer and groan, and La Fonda would say, "There's no rush, baby," as she put one leg up over each arm of the chair so the patrons, her audience, her fans, could see everything.

Universal truth.

Cosmic enlightenment.

Whatever it was that drew them to this place

culminated in a wanting that was akin to worship. They liked to look at her, liked to watch her touch herself with those jet-black fingernails. Oh, she knew what they wanted. She'd smile at them — no words — and then she'd produce a tube of lipstick out of thin air it seemed. She would tart her lips up all candy-apple red and shiny against her wide white teeth. Then she'd lick them, like her fans probably imagined she might lick a lollipop or a lamppost or a tire iron. She'd moan a little, wink at them — because she knew that's exactly what they were thinking — and then she'd reach down to candy-apple gloss that other hole. The one mamma said was dirty.

La Fonda never thought about their lust, though. There would always be "this thing" between them, she said, the way they could just be with each other in silence. They probably all wanted to taste her, of course, smell her, feel her tight skin against theirs. Feel her in a way that made them feel small and ashamed. That kind of hurt is exciting. La Fonda Ian Dark was all things. In that moment, she was everything.

"Fuck. This is bullshit. Boo," they all shouted when the blackout screens came down and the room went pitch and cold. They would ache for her all night, but they'd be with her again soon. "Not soon enough soon, but soon," Larry would always say as he counted the cash in the till. La Fonda was a good earner.

I touched the glass where the image of her had once been. A perfect image, driven from my mind when the buzzer sounded and the little light above the door changed from red to green. I waited — with patience and in silence like I imagined they all did, including my weak-kneed queenistas — one hand on the doorknob, waiting for the latch to click clickety clack open to the dimly lit, red-velvet hall of their youths. They'd all lost it some-where, their innocence, tangled up in all the jasmine-scented pubic hair and lust.

"Next Tuesday?" the stud-boy clerk behind the counter asked me while my pets, the two congealed globs of leathery sweat-juice next to me, giggled and smacked each other.

Did I come here every Tuesday?

"Yes," I shouted at them, and then I asked the clerk to get them a cab before they turned into pumpkin purée. During the subsequent curbside argument over breakfast food, I slipped off to meet Sebastian in what had to be the most certifiably dank-assed dressing room in the known universe, where, like every Tuesday, I would help yank him out of his corset and boots.

By the time we had transformed La Fonda back into her khaki alter ego, the pink smoothness of dawn was upon us, so I called Rita Janine at work, and we all agreed to meet at the open 24-hours diner that was close to the apartment.

AT RISE:
A deserted bus stop, somewhere near Larry's Lush Interiors. 4:00 AM. Sebastian and Girl sit on a bench. The transit advertisement says: BIO-FUELS ARE DRIVING HUNGER. Girl is staring at the newspaper caught in the gutter across the street in front of the all-night launderette, and Sebastian is counting the cigarette butts at his feet. The bus arrives. They board, pay, and find seats.

GIRL:
So, how's the roommate situation?

SEBASTIAN:
Randi has some issues with my career choices.

Randi? That's a new name.

New roommate.

Isn't it the sixth one this year?

Yeah, but I think she'll be the last, and I think next Tuesday might be my last night at Larry Luxe.

What?

Randi is having difficulties with it.

Uh, why does Randall get to have difficulties with your chosen career path?

Randi … and things have gotten sort of serious.

Sort of?

We had sex. Correction: we had amazeballs sex, and now she doesn't think it's appropriate for me to be showing my glory hole to straight perverted strangers.

OK.

She says we are a couple now.

OK.

What am I gonna do, Girl? My whole life has been about the stage. Is the stage. It's the only place I feel truly happy, the only place I can be totally me.

Did you tell her that?

It's not like Broadway is beating down my door. I told her that three shifts at Larry's once a week pays the rent. It does, so I wasn't lying to her.

I think you were.

I know.

I don't know how you do it anyway.

Do what?

How do you do La Fonda? Navigate those shoes? Be who they want you to be?

It's not what *they* want, Girl. I'm not psychic or anything. I have no clue what they want. Don't even care. Probably best not to know, anyway. La Fonda is just another part of me I can set free. Not like a character in a play, but more of a changeling, a magical me that I can experience for a moment … *for me*. It's always for me, Girl. I couldn't do it if it wasn't. Let's get off here and walk the rest of the way. The fella behind us reeks of rum, coke, cherry lube, and ass. I don't like work following me home.

We walked in silence the rest of the way to the diner. I wasn't really contemplating Sebastian's current parole situation, though I probably should have been. I was thinking about Joe. Could I be what he wanted me to be and still be doing it for me? Underline Girl couldn't do it, but maybe I might be able to. I wanted to explore the 'how would I' part of that thought, but I was more concerned with the time and if I could eat, have a decent conversation, and get back to the apartment to tackle the shit, shower, shave situation with enough minutes to spare to make it to work on time, or maybe only late enough that nobody would notice. I didn't actually have to poop, so that would shave off some double digits. I smiled and kicked my pace up a notch when I saw RJ waiving to us through the window of the diner.

Rita Janine and I were roommates at Uni. She has degrees in psychology and philosophy and that led her to nursing school. At first, I didn't understand her desire to be a geriatric nurse. The idea of being surrounded by dead people who didn't seem to know that they were dead, and to do that all day long, seemed morbid and depressing to me, but after spending years with RJ, I came to realize that it had nothing to do with death at all. Well, maybe it did, but in a very abstract sense of the word. RJ has a gift. She has this way about her. A deep elemental softness about her and a flair for decoding ancient languages. She can understand those who can no longer understand themselves. Maybe that's why we connected. Maybe I've always been a charity case.

"Don't you worry about being alone past thirty?" she asked of me, and Sebastian threw her some slick-assed side-eye in acknowledgement, but all I could think about was Joe and the woman in the next booth.

She was eating the biggest piece of cake I'd ever seen at 5:00 in the morning.

I shouldn't have been staring at her, but the entire diner had gone dark, except the light over her table, which somehow seemed a thousand times brighter.

She was all about that cake. The plush red of her lips perfectly poised and parted over a curl of icing.

Why couldn't I be all about the cake? Would Joe want

me to be all about the cake? Should I be wanting to rub icing all over myself? In the morning. In the afternoon. Wherever and whenever there might be an inkling of cake present even in the sale aisle at the market with some old bespectacled clerk in a dirty apron staring at you. Joe's cock might be made of cake. Will I be alone at thirty if I can't get all excited about frosted baked goods?

Where did this conversation even come from? Eggs, bacon, a side of sausage. I remember asking for a second cup of coffee, and I remember the smell of menthol that I had imagined as I watched a man smoke a cigarette out-side on the street — I could use a cigarette — but I don't remember the lead-in or even signing on the dotted line for this topic of discussion. I don't like to think about loneliness. Who obsesses over this? The cake lady didn't care about this. She didn't seem lonely or thirty.

I'm not even close to thirty, and I am not even close to being alone.

I didn't feel alone.

Was I alone?

Shit.

I went home and called in sick from work. I am exceptionally gifted in the subterfuge department, especially when it comes to pretending that I have an incurable disease, like my menstrual cycle. No one wants to die from the plague. No one wants to die from the plague at work, in a cubicle with grey fabric walls and bad fluorescent lighting. It was probably psychosomatic, but I really felt like I had the plague, so I stocked up on supplies: thin mints, sports drink, menthol slims. I pulled on my headlamp and holed myself up in my bedroom closet for the day. Holed myself up with the book, and in so doing, I witnessed, by proxy, a sweaty plethora of people getting pissed on, shit on, tied up, tied down, bathed, diapered, masturbated with electric toothbrushes and/or hands adorned with latex dishwashing gloves, or had their taints massaged with eggbeaters as they were perched precariously, knees in the air, upon the kitchen granite while a day-drinking neighbor in *Speedos* watched with binoculars from across a half-acre of perfectly manicured suburban lawn.

I made that last one up, so why don't I have a gimmick or a thing?

I've got no fucking cake.

I don't have hang-ups either. Nothing. Nada. Zippity do da zilcharoonie.

I am emotionally barren when it comes to this stuff.

In a world where everyone seems to be nakedly embracing their sexuality, some of us prefer a nice big towel. Does that make me the real pervert? A liar when I pretend? Or just a hitchhiker sans a proper towel?

Chapter 9

When Your Only Towel is a Dirty Dish Towel

S peed dating was another one of those things we did when we were bored to tears and out of cash at the end of the month. It's sort of like improvisational comedy. It's fun when you've got a good crowd. If the venue was a bar, and they were offering discounted food and drink, then usually, you'd have a good crowd. Alcohol always makes things funnier than they actually are. Loneliness tends to turn dating into a sport best played while inebriated, the players reduced to cheap appetizers sat upon greasy napkins. Usually the menu offered up oodles of non-gender specific yet thoroughly earned stereotypes, including some of my personal favorites like The Comparison Obsessive, who, like so many other *Playboy* reading ladies' men, can't stop comparing every single woman they meet to the forever unattainable idea of the perfect women they saw slathered to those magazine pages with 24-hour deep restoring hand lotion. Then we have the Rebound Douche, who starts blubbering at even the slightest idle mention of his recent breakup, which he can't stop mentioning and was exactly two years ago on this very day, no matter the day. Or if you prefer spicier bites, we have: the Clingy Jailer, so don't even think about not responding to their text immediately; or, the Can't Get Over Their Ex who shattered their ego into tiny perfect shards of vomit-tinted glass; and, my personal favorite, the Narcissistic Twat Boy whose detailed facial cleansing and early morning glute-toning ritual will be more excruciatingly painful than the torture one might have experienced during the Spanish Inquisition, torture that he is probably planning for you when he finishes his sixth vanilla vodka martini, if he can get you down into his basement. There's probably a story about a rescue dog in there somewhere, so be mindful.

I don't really know what muscles you're supposed to flex during this nonsense, but it should be called speed gagging. Now, I'm never in this for real and neither are Matt, Bitch, and Rita Janine. It's just fun. Sometimes to waste away an afternoon, and sometimes, we make new friends. We try to do all kinds of crazy things. It's almost like a masquerade ball. One time we all put on fake British accents and spent the evening saying *fuck all* and *cunt* a lot. Sebastian used to come with us, but La Fonda would have us all giggling so much that none of us could stay on point for very long, so we banned him. I can't deal with distractions because I like to have a game plan in advance. A disguise. A persona. A fake me and a list of absurdities to test the resolve of even the most seasoned speeders. Since I don't have any quantifiable experience in the dating department, I see it as a social experiment even if it's mostly for my own amusement. I want to see what reaction I'll get asking all the wrong questions.

How do like my boobs? (Squeezes boobs into better positioning.) I'm thinking of having my nipples removed. Yeah, like *Barbie.* Would that work for you? My nip rings got caught in someone's dental work, so I was thinking, who needs them anyway.

Sorry, I'm a little gun shy. My last boyfriend tied me up and then accidentally set a motel room on fire when he tried to strap a butane torch to his penis. Do you dig S&M? Maybe just the M? I have to stop at the hardware shop after this, wanna come with?

How many people have *you* had sex with? Bet my list is way longer.

Where were you thinking we'd have sex later? I know this great pet cemetery. Mortuary works too.

Or, I'd just get piss-faced drunk and ask them about kids or money. Ask them if I could meet their mom later, or could I friend them on social media, cuz you know, we *can* be friends.

You have to do that last one with creepy stalker side-eye. Helps to practice in the bathroom mirror first.

Since Underline Girl came into my life, I've changed up my questions some, and my attitude about a lot of apparently meaningless crap. These dating situations can be meat markets, and you do cross paths with a lot of hook-up psycho and cheater types. I didn't think Matt or anybody would ever cheat on me. Yes, there is such a thing as friend cheating. We've all known each other for a long time, so we are all good at filtering out potential losers and usurpers from our friend group, or so I thought until Mathilda.

We met Mathilda at a feminist-goth mingle. She was a country girl, rough, the way a rusted combine that's been sitting out in a field of cow shit is. Mathilda was slag pits, rattlers, mule stink, cheap beer, and wind through shabby clapboards, so she didn't care. About anything. She frequents dark places. Buys stuff at organic markets and talks about Morocco like she'd just unpacked her suitcase yesterday. I'm ordinary compared to that. Non-specific. Nothing about me, even my made-up shit, is that remotely interesting. I've never been to Morocco or anywhere really other than the Podunk Hallow Matt and I grew up in. It's OK though. Mathilda plays the cello. Lives in a crack-shack near the Jade Fountain take-out. They use snakes and stray cats in their *lo mein*. That fact isn't in the Jesus book, she says, but everyone around here knows those people eat snakes and stray cats. Mathilda says she feels interfered with. Spoiled. From the snakes and the cello and the smell come from the kitchen at that Jade Fountain shithole. She says she wishes that she could just peel her skin off and put it in a scrapbook, as a souvenir. Bitch said she'd like to paint Mathilda's skin. Mathilda likes whiskey. I don't like whiskey. All I have is apologies, rats, cockroaches, and right now, maybe those Jesus snakes in my veins. Mathilda says she has them too. She picks at hers till they bleed.

"She called me a Nubian princess."

"She asked me where Gomez was."

"She just laughed at me. You think it was my hat?"

In Matt's case, I was sure it was his hat; however, when I asked, "So, who's gonna call her?" I discovered in the end that every one of them already had her digits on speed dial. Nothing worse than being righteously out-done at your own game.

It was several months into the whole Mathilda thing when I caught Matt wearing a thong.

Innocent enough, we were doing the usual, shelving the newest influx of books when Matt bent over in front of me and there it was, that cheeky bit of string.

"Hey Matt, if you were a plumber, you'd be rockin' way better bank than you do working here."

"What the hell are you going on about now, Girl? You gotta stop conversating in your head."

"I'm talking about the sex-ay new look you got going on. If you want a good time, call Miracle Matt at 1-900-flossmahcrack."

He flipped me off.

Apparently, Mathilda told him that his chakras were clogged or some other mystic voodoo snake oil crap, and that he should ditch his lifelong appreciation for flannel boxers, so I asked him if things felt airier down there, to which he replied that things had got more interesting but that he wasn't sold on the whole string up his butt thing yet. Mathilda is so cliché that I'm surprised she didn't try to get him into garters.

There were other little changes too. Subtle things that got under my skin. Matt started going to a stylist for his hair. A fucking stylist. For years, I'd always cut his hair with the kitchen shears and it didn't cost fifty bucks. He bought mouthwash and tooth whitener. Polished his boots. Put patches on the holes in his jeans and cologne on his crotch instead of the bug spray.

Cologne on his crotch. Seriously.

Then he went on for twenty minutes about her damn freckles. I'm talking wit's end here, piss on my fence post shit. She had all these tiny little freckles all over her face. The kind I wanted to draw little hearts around and then play connect the dots with an *X-Acto* knife. Next thing I knew, Matt was hovering over me with his hand out.

"What?"

"Here. You were mumbling something about needing an *X-Acto* knife."

I was losing my mind. Losing my friends. Losing my best friend to freckles and Jesus snakes and stupid-assed Moroccan cocktails.

This wasn't *Scrabble* or bowling. I was losing time.

Matt was going to yoga with Mathilda. Going to paint-n-sip with Mathilda. Going to martini bars and strip clubs with Mathilda. Why not just go to hell with her too? I had to hack his phone to get Duncan's number, because bug spray or no bug spray, I actually needed a new friend, and one with dreary old vinyl seemed like the mentholated salve I so desperately needed.

Mathilda had infiltrated every aspect of my life. Rita Janine and Bitch couldn't stop talking about her. She could paint like Bob Ross. She used to be on a roller derby team, and did you know, she made five-hundred bucks beating everyone at The Blue Buick playing pool last Thursday night during the manic midnight happy hour.

I was home Thursday night. Alone.

I'm not a paranoid person, generally, so in a show of

good faith and solidarity, Matt and I went to dinner with
Mathilda a bunch of times, and every single time, I felt
like I was being choked to death with my own intestines.

Mathilda is sad all the time.

Sad for no good reason.

Punch my fist through the back of her head sad and
pathetic and miserable.

All. The. Time.

Except when she listens to the radio. She does like to
listen to the radio. She says it calms her down when she
can imagine herself inside the songs, inside even the bad
ones. The reds change to blues and the electric whites in
her eyes to infinite greys just knowing that in roughly
three minutes the story will be over. She says she likes the
idea of being over. She's tried, she says. It's not that
simple. Me, I wanted to disappear too. Slowly. From
knowing her. Mathilda smiled at me and then licked her
food, Matt's food, and then she turned to scout out
anyone else's food left unattended. It was embarrassing.
She chews her nails and dresses for shit too, like an anime
schoolgirl sat eating scabs in a fine restaurant next to a
giant dung beetle in a billycock and six-fold. Matt's the
beetle. I tried not to look across the table at her. All the
food and the booze and the chintz-covered walls closing
in on me were making me sweat. She was making me
sweat, so I told her that I was sad too, which at that
moment was totally true, then I wondered if I could make
a noose from the frayed seam thread in my pocket that I'd
been playing with so that I might pull the half-chewed
food out of my throat when I started choking like I always
do in public when I am sweaty, nervous, and irritated.
Knock. Knock. Who's there? Girl. Fidgety, sweaty, crazy-

eyed Girl. Or maybe it's the habaneros in my pilaf.

"Are you OK?" Matt asked me in a stern whisper, but all I could do was watch Mathilda as she shoved a fistful of knuckle into her mouth, so Matt had to say it again, "Girl! Are you OK?"

There really are too many people. In the room. In the world. "It's a Tuesday night. I'm OK, but why are there so many people? That man's elbow is literally in my plate. Literally. Do you think they know how crowded it is? The management. It feels crowded, don't you think?"

"I don't know, and I don't care. What difference does it make that it's Tuesday? You don't even know these people, Girl, so can you please just —"

I cut him off because I hate Mathilda, but I love Matt, so I stopped myself before I said what I wanted to say. The waiter filled my wine glass. He was smirking.

Twice Mathilda and I had the antibiotic-injected steak and the bitter-almond torte here. This time it was radio-active squid and Vietnamese coffee jelly. Mathilda smells like a meadow. The cab driver had a picture of one on his visor. Old Country. That's my memory of her now, in this moment: a black cab, billowing exhaust fumes on a hill in a Romanian meadow. I stand in the kitchenette at Matt's place, feet cold against the tile. Her voice echoes up the staircase, crushes my lungs when I inhale it over the whiskey in my hand. I'm afraid of what might happen to us if I leave. If I manage somehow to control the twisting and the spinning left without balance, will there still be a Matt? Will there still be a me? What if?

I just want everything to be normal again. Matt lying next to me, drunk, shivering under the covers at three in the morning. I want to punch the shit out of Mathilda.

Over the uneaten squid and all the bags of vomit she tries to hide in the basement? Tries to hide from me.

I know what you're doing, Mathilda. I know.

The only intimate time I could get with Matt these days was time spent working in the bookshop, but that was probably because I'd gotten brick dust from the local chemist and sprinkled it over all the entrances and windowsills. Matt couldn't understand where all the red footprints were coming from, and I just grinned a deep internal loathing type grin, the sort you do when you hate someone and secretly know you've gotten the better of them in some small and petty way. I can do a respectable small and petty, and it's a hell of a lot better than gnawing on my own fingernails.

The whole thing was hard to swallow because I was so caught up with vague and unknown variables. Was my relationship with Matt ending? Had our friendship reached its peak? Was Mathilda a legitimate reason to mourn? What was I mourning? Maybe a hypnotist could put me under and get to the dank inside my head. At the very least, maybe they could help me equate Mathilda with liverwurst sandwiches or something else other than hate.

I need to feel, process, resist…

There's cat hair in my eye.

There's this pressure in my chest all time.

Where are you, Joe? I think I need you.

Chapter 10

It's Complicated, A Life Status

I did not know that this sex thing was so complicated, so involved. "It's more than just blowing your wad then? I don't mean to be gross or stupid, it's just that I've never, you know, never had one."

"One what, Girl? Ladies blow gaskets, not wads."

"You know what I mean. You're gonna make me say it aren't you? That I've never had an orgasm. There. I said it. I confess." I thought that maybe being open to the Jesus snakes Mathilda always talked about would help me reconnect with Matt. The book had dropped some serious knowledge and confidence on me, but I only felt a crushing sense of failure right after my life-sans-orgasm confession. Matt didn't seem surprised by my admission and proceeded to comfort me in a way that didn't make me feel like a turnip that had gone off.

"Well, that's not that unusual, considering that most men, in bed, are selfish cunts or just daft. Sometimes they're both, and many women are simply afraid of their own bodies. There's all this conflict of interest."

"I wouldn't know anything about interest."

"What about all those men in college, at the clubs, at parties? You left with them?"

"Sure, but nothing happened except maybe coffee, midnight pastry, and polite conversation."

"What about all the dildos and vibrators?"

"Those are Bitch and Rita Janine's."

"You've never tried one?"

"No. I thought I might. Turned one on once, but it was just so intimidating, like a power tool. My whole arm was vibrating. I just couldn't."

"Couldn't or wouldn't?"

This time I had to think about the question, because this time, I really didn't know.

"Look, Girl, I'm gonna say something here, and I don't want you getting all squinty thinking I am trying to impose anything on you or make you feel harassed or something equally ridiculous, but aren't you at least a little curious? You say you don't feel normal type stuff when it comes to sex, and I get that, but how can you say you're not normal if you have no experience to back up the assumption? Maybe the way you feel about sex, or don't feel about it, is perfectly normal and right, and maybe the crazy animalistic way everyone else seems to feel about it is abnormal. Or maybe it's all normal. Damn.

I guess I'm trying to say that you, in your very particular position at this time, can't possibly gauge what normal is or isn't."

"What about getting peed on?"

"Seriously? Like a Golden shower?"

"Yeah. Is that normal?"

"Girl, you know I gag in public toilets, and I get queasy when Sendak pees in the litterbox in front of me, so maybe it's normal for some, but not for me. Normal is subjective. Look, I get it. You don't want to be one of those old ladies who masturbate with an electric toothbrush. That is a *Lysol* situation for sure."

"So what then, Matt, are you offering — again?"

"No! Oh God no. You gotta walk first, right. I know I tease you all the time about us doing it, but I'm being totally serious now. As your best friend. No coitus. Just an orgasm."

He said that I was his best friend, and that he wants to give me something. Just a small gesture. Shit. How was he going to accomplish that without sexing me up?

"Oh, Girl. Girl. Girl. Girl. You had the magic wand in your hand, and you just chickened out. You can try again. I'll help you so you're not so afraid."

"I'm not afraid." I just didn't get past the pee chapter in the book yet.

"Yes, you are."

OK, maybe I was a little scared. Not of the thing itself, but maybe, I was afraid of not liking it at all. Ever. The disappointment. The failure. Mathilda telling him that he should have given up on me ages ago. She probably has six orgasms at a time and cries afterwards. I have a thirty-thousand word vocabulary, according to some interwebz test. I don't live in *Candyland*. I know that something happens when you stick your finger up a guy's butthole. So there Mathilda. Take that...

And we went back to my place.

Bitch and Rita Janine were with Mathilda at some kind of gothic performance art show, and so I had the place to myself for once. It was dark and quiet and I was nervous, so I spent a long time in the bathroom looking for chin hair to pluck and other imperfections to pick at, then I spent a longer amount of time sitting on the toilet sipping wine, smoking a joint, and contemplating global warming while I tried to decide if I should get under the bed sheets to take off my underwear or if I should stand tall and just let them slide and flick off my toe like the ladies do in those make-believe movie strip-clubs. Somehow, like one does in astral projection situations, I finally ended up in the bedroom, and I'd probably been standing there zipping and unzipping my jeans for about ten minutes when Matt finally blew a gasket and said, "I've seen your vagina before."

"Not since we were ten."

"Damn it, Girl, how different could it look?"

"Still gross."

"Yeah, I'm sure it is ... and hairy."

"Not hairy."

"What do you mean?"

"I get it done."

"What? Like at the barber? Take a little off the top and blow it out 70s retro."

"No! For shit's sake, Matt. I get it waxed. Bitch does it for me, and it's all your fault anyway. Those stupid *Playboy* magazines. Pubes freak me out."

"All-righty then, so it's gross and bald. Whatever. You're just stalling, now take them off."

So, I did. He watched with his hands on his hips, and I felt worse than exposed. Everything felt cold, and when I sat down on the edge of the bed, my comforter felt like a burlap sack lined with fiberglass and tacks.

Matt dimmed the lights, told me to lie down, and then he lay down beside me, close so he could hold my one shaking hand and whisper in my ear that everything was going to be all right. That he would talk me through it and that there was nothing to feel weird or afraid about. I didn't actually believe him, but I did trust him. It might have been his soft soapy smell or the way his stylishly coiffed hair brushed against my cheek, whatever it was, I felt safe … in that small space between the idea of each other and the reality of it all … safe, staring up at the ceiling, trying not to laugh.

"Good Lord, Girl. Is my majestic manhood not enough for you? What are you? Twelve? Adults don't put posters on their ceilings, let alone over the bed."

"Hey now. Don't get down on the *Boosh*, and I thought Vince Noir was your fashion idol?"

"Uh, no."

"Sorry, I forgot. You cultivate your own thing."

"Hey. Looking this fabulous all the time takes work not plagiarism, and you're stalling again."

"No, I'm not—"

Then the vibrator came out. This huge hulking rubber mallet of destruction in neon purple glory, and when he turned it on, it made that chunk sound like when the power comes back on after an outage. I expected the lights to flicker and auxiliary power sirens to start blaring somewhere off in the distance. I didn't even want to touch it. Wasn't sure if Bitch had washed it since its last use, so I thought I might get tetanus, if you can get tetanus from latex, or maybe there was lead in the neon purple colorant. It was probably made in China, and they put lead in everything for good measure. Matt just sighed, squeezed my hand a bit harder, and said I was just being ridiculous, but I didn't think I was, then it occurred to me, "I'll get carpal tunnel."

"You won't."

"Look at that fucking thing?"

"I know. Some of the stuff they had in that cupboard made *me* sweaty. We're talking medieval torture devices. Steam-punk meets alien nation. I can hear the advertisement now: EXPERIENCE ALIEN CREATURE SCHLONG. ACHIEVE ORGASM AND TIME TRAVEL. SIX SETTINGS WILL TAKE YOU TO EUPHORIC GALAXIES FAR AND WIDE." We both started laughing, and I could barely breathe, but suddenly, with him laughing and the poster of Vince Noir over the bed smiling down at me in anticipation, I realized that the entire situation wasn't funny anymore.

"What if I make those faces?"

"What faces?"

"You know, those embarrassing contorted porn faces."

"You won't. I don't even know what you're talking about, Girl, but you won't."

"What if I do? You can't guarantee that I won't, and I don't want you to see me all freakishly twisted up like a carnival sideshow exhibit," and with that came the exasperated grunt I was waiting for, the one that usually indicates that I had won the battle and that whatever issue we were debating would soon get chucked in the too-tired-to-argue-about-it bin.

"OK. OK. I'll close my eyes. Now can we just get on with it?"

Matt put the vibrator in my hand, told me where to put it, how to move it around, and then he closed his eyes … for the duration.

I was seriously concerned with electrocution. It sort of felt like it at the start, and in the middle, and at the end when parts unknown began convulsing. I totally understood what might happen if an executioner had forgotten to wet the sponge for your head and then fired up *yellow mama* without giving it a second thought. I was burning up from the inside out. Well, the parts of me that weren't totally numb. What also surprised me was how quickly the whole thing came and went. I looked over at Matt, who still had his eyes closed, and I asked if that was it?

He opened one eye tentatively to make sure the situation wasn't still volatile. It wasn't, as I had already pulled the sheet over my crotch, and so he smiled and sat up on one elbow. "No, Girl. That's not all of it. It's said to be much better if you have one of those during actual sex with someone you actually care about. You know, there's more … other stuff … but, well, it doesn't really matter, does it — to you?"

But for some reason, right then, it did. I don't know why. I don't know if I even liked it. What I did like was the way he was still holding my hand, and before I knew it, we were ten again, giggling in our bramble fort.

"Why don't you stay?"

"I can't, I have to feed Sendak."

"He'll be OK. He'll eat a rat or something."

"I don't want him eating those funky contaminated rats, Girl. I really have to go. I'll see you tomorrow at the shop."

The leaving part was always uncomfortable for us, especially if one of us was in a vulnerable state. This time was no different, and Matt's fumbling stumbling departure was the slog of the century. He couldn't find his shoes. Then his hat. Then his keys. Then the bedroom door, finding the only closet and then the bathroom before the third attempt proved the correct choice. I wanted to say something to him, but what could I say about what had just happened? That it felt relaxing, and yet, not. I couldn't admit that it only felt sort of OK because it didn't. Nothing felt OK. Not before. Not during. And most certainly not now. I couldn't find the courage to say anything because I didn't want Matt to think that he had done something wrong. I didn't want him to know that I felt wrong. That the something I did feel had widened into a gaping septic hole in my chest. How could I tell him that I didn't really want that? That I wanted something different. Something else. Something deeper. Something beyond whatever this was, so I couldn't find the courage to say anything, and I couldn't do anything except sink further into the mattress until I could feel the metal springs poking me in the ass.

Eventually, he left.

The front door slammed shut.

And I felt alone.

Itchy, sweaty, confused, and alone.

I wanted to hit something, and I wanted to scream. Horror movie scream until I could find the strength, at least, to cry. Joe wouldn't have left me like this:

Damaged.

Lonely.

Wanting.

If only Joe were here.

Underline Girl doesn't deserve you, Joe.

And it's late...

Too late to inventory the streaks in my eyeliner, but I really want to go out. Are you waiting for me, Joe? In a bar. A dive. It's cliché that you would be, but I really don't care. I just want to be with someone. With you. Somewhere, maybe anywhere. Somewhere on the way, out of the way, in the night, in the filth and shadows. I put on stockings; lace up boots; look at the twists in my legs reflected in the mirror.

I imagine you, Joe, a cocktail in your hand, an Old Fashioned maybe, something pretentious — something sepia varnished in black and white — as you wait for me, a slight smile on your face, the dim bar light a minute imperfection in your eye.

It's not about how I imagine you, imagine me, or how I imagine you're with me when you're not or that you might like that cardigan I thought about buying last week but didn't.

It's not about how I imagine us together, Joe. When I'm alone. Now. Lipstick on the wineglass. I sip slowly; watch myself smoke in the mirror. The swirls of mentholated air spilling over my lips lift and frame my face in acid strokes of brutal mystery, but only for a moment. A moment I'll forget in a moment.

When I close my eyes, I think I can feel you, Joe, if your hands were here and maybe there. Skin pressed to skin. Lips. Whispers. Darkness soft and forgiving. We could be strangers to each other, to ourselves, coalescing in the never had, never wanted, never needed to be.

But I feel empty inside.

And your hands are nowhere.

I think about sleeping, not sleeping, and why I'm not sleeping and maybe you are. I imagine daydreaming about sleeping while watching you twist yourself into the folds of my sheets. Twist yourself into the folds of time I imagine might not be real. I think that, maybe, I could forget you in my dreams.

Maybe.

But right now, Joe, I can't find the momentum to do anything except imagine that it's all much easier with than without you … haunting me.

Chapter 11

Endings

S aturday, boxes, unpacking, but this time, I didn't take the bus all the way to the bookshop. I only took two of my transfers and decided to walk the rest of the way. I really needed the time to think about what had happened last night before I had to look Matt in the face all casual like as if nothing unduly weird had gone on. Turns out, I didn't have to worry about it much. Matt wouldn't look me in the eye, and the level of silence was astonishing, considering that the two of us had always had trouble shutting our cake-holes ... but there it was, that awesomely gelatinous silence, dripping off everything in the shop.

We drank coffee in silence.

Smoked a couple of joints in silence, which takes an ungodly amount of skill.

We ate Chinese in silence, which for Matt, also takes an ungodly amount of skill, and we each, respectively, even pet Sendak in silence.

Sendak didn't mind, but I did.

There was so much silence that I thought I could hear the noodles shifting around in the takeout container like puked-up tapeworms.

Boxes, books, shelves. Boxes, books, shelves. The only faintly audible sound was that of our shoes shuffling against the hairy grit on the floor.

My head was pounding from the not-noise and all the disjointed rust-riddled thoughts clinking and clanking against each other in my head, when all of a sudden, I wondered what Joe would have done in the situation?

"What situation?"

I was glad he spoke first, or maybe I had. It didn't really matter. There were sounds and words out there now. In that sticky, rubbery air. "You know. What we did last night. I wonder if Joe would have been so calm about it and if he would have stayed the night, you know, for moral support." I felt confident in the articulation of what had been only jumbled thoughts in my head a moment ago, and I smiled at Matt, but the response that was levelled at me had just about the same velocity and impact as a brick does when it's dropped from five stories up directly towards your face.

"Look, Girl, I wanted to stay, but I couldn't because … I want something different. Hey. Don't cross your arms at me. I get that sex doesn't mean anything to you. I get it. I get you, and I don't care, because it doesn't matter to me, either. You can side-eye me all you want but that's how I feel. I don't know what's going on with you lately, and I think it's time to have a discussion because I think you are starting to swerve at the wheel a bit. Girl, let me finish. I want to have a real discussion. Not an argument. Not one of your circular segues through a psych ward, just a nice chill discussion about what happened last night. Alright? OK, then.

"We did this thing, Girl. This ridiculously intimate thing and you say nothing. That look on your face when you asked me to stay. I don't know if it's the stupid book, or this obsession you have with this make-believe Joe, but I felt like you were coerced into doing something that you didn't really want to do. It felt like I coerced you, so I bailed because I felt guilty."

"Seriously, Matt. Guilty for what?"

"For teasing you all these years. For making you think you had to change to please me. For all my misguided sexual rhetoric."

"You don't make me think or do anything, Mattie—"

"Girl, please let me finish...

"You know I don't care about money, or trendy clothes, or high-end cocktails, or fancy manicures, but I do care about kissing, about caring, about cuddling. I care about real intimacy, and you know that making the first move isn't my thing. I think casual sex is a dangerous waste of time, that romance is forever, and that everyone who talks about their sex life is a self-aggrandizing ass. Everyone, including me. I've only been with three women. One. Two. Fucking Three. That's it. I don't think sex is all that important, either, and I've never had sex with Mathilda. I'm only saying that because I know you're going to ask and because, for some reason, she gets under your skin like a rabid chigger."

His number three middle finger was still pointing in my general direction when I said, "You lied? I can't believe you lied." It was a stupid thing to say because maybe, probably, I've been lying to myself in thinking that all this sexual enlightenment wasn't just a big fat biological joke, but right then, the fact that maybe, probably, I was a hypocrite escaped me. Matt wasn't a liar. I knew in my heart that he was just screwing around with me, like he always does.

"No, you assume things all the time, Girl. The fact that I don't correct you because I think it's funny doesn't exactly mean that I'm lying. Hyperbole isn't lying, but it feels the same. I've been screwing with you all this time, but I'm not right now. If you want to assume I lied, about it all, then fine, but don't give me that shock-awe raised eyebrow nonsense either. You know exactly what I'm talking about. You know I talk trash. When I'm with Duncan or Bitch, we talk about dicks; we talk about porn; we talk about dildos and porn. Is it length or width that matters with said dildos? We talk about how often we masturbate — a lot — and how often we masturbate to porn — not in front of each other, obviously. We talk about how much we hate fakers who say they hate porn. And yoga. Fuck Chakras. WE hate yoga. These are the sort of relevant irrelevant questions that fashionable modern men such as myself and Duncan's self need answered. Girl, we've been together forever. You're my best friend, and sometimes, I talk trash because I forget who you really are, and when I do, remember that you are not Duncan or Bitch, I feel like crap for teasing you. I lie when I have to. Sometimes I lie a lot, and it kills me, but I still can't tell you the truth because you don't want to hear the truth. I love you, but your lens is righteously warped. You only hear and see what's in your own made up narrative."

"The clubbing?"

"You know Duncan and I hate clubbing. You always look like you're having so much fun with the girls or the queens, so Duncan and I leave to go down to The Blue Buick, or we go to his place to get stoned."

"The speed-date digits?"

"Never called a single one. Same as you apparently. Well, no, that's not true, *you* called Mathilda first."

"Yeah, what about Mathilda? Come on now. You can't lie about Mathilda."

"She's been helping me work through something. That's all."

"I bet, Matt. Work through that something different you say you want. I bet you both work really hard at it."

"Girl, I've only had sex with three women and only because I thought they were the one. It was college, and I was a stupid kid. They weren't the one. I know who the real one is. I want someone who gets me. Like you have since we were ten years old. But lately, I don't get you. I've been trying to compete with some fictitious idea you've got in your head since that book. Trying to be something you are not is as uncomfortable as those thong underpants. I know that now, thanks to Mathilda, and I'm fine with it. Joe isn't real. He's just some insecure girl's projection. Her naive idea of a boyfriend cleverly draped over some gas lighting bullshit. He's probably just a normal guy who didn't *get* her particular brand of crazy. I want to be me, and I want you to be you. I want everything back the way it was ... with us. Fuck Joe. Fuck sex. Just fuck it. None of this nonsense is real. Now where's that goddamned book? I've had enough of it, enough of your asinine, guilt-obsessed sex fantasy," and with that he full-body lunged over the counter and tore the backpack out of my hand before I had a chance to swing it out of his reach. While I was just standing there with my mouth open, the book flew out, landed, and then skidded across the hairy floor. We both looked at each other with venom and grit teeth; then Matt darted and took a slide, kicking the book out of my reach. Shit fell off shelves. Sendak's kibble tin flew into the wall. Kibble in my hair, I fell on my face rather spectacularly when I dove for the book, which was so clearly out of my reach. My elbow hit the metal frame on one of the shelves and it hurt so bad that I doubled up into a fetal knot of silent screaming. Matt simply replied with a confident, "Ha!" as he crawled off into the corner to retrieve the prize, and in a stumbling, shrieking, blur of flailing hands and insults, the book, *my book* — the Underline Girl, Joe, all the secrets — would wind up in the alley-can out back, doused with butane, and set alight with Matt dancing psychotically around the can as if he were making a sacrifice to Satan. I scrabbled out to the alley, clutching my wounded arm, but I was too late. All I could do was stand there and watch the flames lick higher and higher as wild-eyed pyro Matt continued to squirt butane into the can while Sendak watched from his brick outpost above us, a mouse in his mouth, an I-told-you-so in his beautiful blue eyes.

I felt drained.

Maybe even a little betrayed.

"I'm calling Mathilda," I said with a heartbroken coldness I didn't know I had in me. "She'll know what to do with you, because, well, I don't anymore."

"Oh, that's rich, Girl. I've been saying the same thing to her about you. Why are you so exasperating? Go ahead. Call her. She'll say the same thing I'm going to say to you now: She's is not my girlfriend. *You are.* Always have been, you nitwit."

I really didn't have any thoughts or feelings about Matt's last statement other than recognition relevant to the unpleasant dryness that seemed to be crawling across my tongue. I was at a loss for pithy words, at a loss for breath, so I went with gasping flinty instead: "Fuck you Matt, and fuck you too, Sendak. I'm going home."

I actually felt relieved. That the book was gone. That I was a nitwit, and that Mathilda was nothing more than a girl who did yoga. One cannot not admit nitwit status in a fuck-off moment though, so 'Going Home' was the best I could come up with. In light of my crushing defeat, I really wasn't in the mood for romantic vagaries and stupid relationship idiocy, so I stomped back into the shop, kicked and fussed through the mess of words and kibble on the floor until I found my backpack, then I headed out towards the bus stop.

Chapter 12

The Perfect Paradigm

S o there was this bench, wood, birdshit, nothing special about it. Just a bench on which we were sat. Waiting. Fall leaves in a swirling vortex at our feet. Dust and naked trees. Cooing winged rats all around us.

Just a bench on a street.

Just a girl.

Just a guy.

I'm the girl, and I had this thought. I'm really no good at thoughts, and usually, I get what I deserve when I have them. I'm kinda like the bench. Matt isn't. He's just a guy. A guy I know. A guy I love despite his lack of fashion sense. When he sat down beside me, I'd been looking into this little compact mirror, which I had extricated from my backpack with great difficulty only moments before. I was looking into it all squint-eyed as I smeared and smeared and smeared my lips with color. That's when the thought came to me, so I put it out there in frustration, "Why do I, well, why do women put this stuff on their lips." There was no question mark there because it really wasn't a question. Just a why bother sort of statement. I stopped the smearing long enough to look at Matt and smile. Then I went back to the task at hand. Smear, smear, smear, pucker, pucker, pucker, smear, smear, smear. "I don't get it, you know. I think I have pretty lips. Most women have pretty lips, not that I stalk women's lips or anything. I'm not saying that. I'm just asking. Do you think I have pretty lips?" This time it was a genuine question mark, and in return, I got a smile from Matt that was a lot like the bench. I snapped the mirror shut, chucked it and the lipstick into my backpack, and then I turned to face him with lips that I imagined looked a lot like those huge wax lips you get to eat at Halloween time. Matt probably thought so too but didn't say as much for very obvious reasons, and so there was this little bit of silence until he blew me a kiss with a "You really want to know?" attached to it. I did, and "I do," was my reply because the bench and the birdshit and the pecking rats were all getting on my nerves and I was cold and benches don't get cold, so that was odd, and he just looked at me like I was odd and said, very calmly, "Fellatio," and that's why I'm the bench and he is not. I wanted him to kiss me. Wanted him to want to kiss me. It was a thought I'd had last night when I was thinking of Joe, but I didn't want Joe to kiss me, or hold my hand, or anything. I told Matt as much, and I asked for a tissue, but then my bus came and I wasn't sure if I could wait any longer for him or the tissue, even if he had one.

After the bus pulled away and the cloud of noxious smog had cleared, there was this bench: wood, birdshit, nothing special about it. Just a bench on which we were sat. Just a girl and a guy.

I AM GIRL.

Joe could never be Matt, and Matt is my guy. Always has been, apparently.

While I was contemplating the truth in that along with the scuffs on my boots, Matt slipped his hand into mine, nudged me with his shoulder, and, as he stared at nothing in particular in the distance, he said that we'd figure it out.

I stopped staring at my shoes long enough to catch a quick glimpse of his hand in mine, and I realized that, maybe, this is just the way it's done.

About the Author

Cheryl Anne Gardner is a writer of dark, often disturbing art-house novellas and abstract flash fiction. Her love of literature began at an early age with Stoker's Dracula. Captivated by the Gothic and Dark Romantic stylings of Poe, Lovecraft, Kafka, and de Sade, her passion for the macabre manifests itself throughout her own work to this day. In 2010, she became enamored with Flash Fiction and its experimental style, and she's been writing prolifically in the genre ever since. She enjoys exploring political, social, and psychological issues. Her flash fiction has been published in dozens of journals. When she isn't writing, she likes to chase marbles on a glass floor, eat lint, play with sharp objects, and make taxidermy dioramas with dead flies. She lives with her husband on the east coast USA, is an enthusiastic gardener, and dabbles in cement sculpture when she isn't spoiling her adopted feral cats.

You can find her work at various online retailers. Her novellas are available in print and in eBook formats.

Titles by Cheryl Anne Gardner

Kitsch
The Duskhouse
And Death Dreamt Us All
The Thin Wall
Logos
The Splendor of Antiquity
The Kissing Room

A Lukewarm Glass of Milk

S he liked eating the lint she found under the furniture cushions. Liked chewing the paint off the bedpost when we made love. Everything was always beginning with her. Predawn. Fresh cut flowers sans the morning dew. She was double-jointed, and when she hit me, she said it was just a reflex.

"I can't find my jacket. You know, the brown one with the fancy leather flowers on the lapels," she said, and then she gave me the stink-eye as she cut a banana into her morning cereal.

The sun was just coming in through the kitchen window, and when it lit on her, her whole face sparkled from the pancake makeup she always applied too thickly. She said her life was in miniature, carved of Chinese jade then photographed in black and white and tacked to a light post in a parking lot. Everything was brilliant to her, always in the fake British accent she'd learned from watching too many foreign films. She sipped her coffee, said I wasn't flexible anymore. I told her, "The jacket is in the basement closet." I'd put it there because it stunk of cigarette smoke, even though she'd said she quit. The newspaper says the forecast for today will be hazy with a heat index of 101 degrees. I don't understand the heat index. How do they know how hot it feels to me?

(2012, August). Blue Fifth Notebook.

Ditch Diggers Tend Picket Fences

S ilence spreads into space, upstream in nuclear steel and chrome comfort. There's a bottle of gin on the floor that should be empty but it's not, and an argument under the table that shouldn't be but is. He'd tried to escape but couldn't, and she asked for it — with question marks. Told him that his ellipses were obscene, and then she cried briefly to survive him.

"So I'll stay," he said, again, and she told him to bury it out next to the shed. There's a maple tree there, listing against the wind, so he put on his gumboots and carried it out there alone with gin hands bare. Shaking. The shed door rots, protests, and the coal shovel's rusted out. A life lived in short seasons, he thinks, as he stabs the earth with a clank only to realize that he couldn't break ground even if he tried, and he's tried so many times, but the soil is sour. She knows that. The daisies she plants die every year. She won't be perfect or right or wonderful, he will never not be ignorant, and the daisies will always fucking die. Without argument. Without question marks.

Once, he painted a green field, she standing in it, the wind in her hair and in the lace hems of her dress. She cut the skin from her breast and gave it to him. He set his hair on fire and gave her the ash. They made love in the moonlight, that field now gray, and as he pressed his thumbs into her throat, she asked him a question, but he can't remember what it was. Then she said she wished she had a glass eye, one that would never grow hazy when she looked at him, like the marbles they'd played with on the street when they were kids. He had one in his pocket just for such an occasion. She laughed and she laughed, and she laughed ... until she didn't.

It used to be you and me.

We.

Us.

Now it's just He. She. Them. Always kneeling there, under that tree in the dead dirt, praying for something ... anything at all. Hoping for an emptiness she can live with: a hole deep enough for all his regret.

(2015, February). Change Seven Magazine

Desperate Islands are Ours

I find you, sitting in a piazza at a cafe table, alone, a dusky bowl of prime opaque in front of you, served with a side of sticky bacon and gin. "Soon," you say to me, but you always say soon when I'm late, so I tap my foot and wait while squids serenade us from a balcony above; then, after a brief violin concerto and a careless "thank you mister" to God for all the small matters he's chosen to ignore, we ride raindrops on eucalyptus dust, lace handkerchiefs crumpled in our pockets. I only fear you when you're near me. I want to tell you that, but just then, the waiter arrives with a stone tablet. You pay the bill with a fist full of coin and ask if the pharmacy's open all night. It is, so you make mental notes in time and shadow while walking behind me in irritation as I foretell the future in condescending rivulets, my rubber boots flip, flap, flopping against a sunset that isn't ours … and never will be.

(2014, March) ExFic

Spider Cocktails Lilt in Icy Hands

C ast down, your shadowed eyes he tolerates, barely but patiently, as luncheonette counters reflect polished shards of spit and grease into his own. Your voice is an echo, ones and zeros in a noxious void, and it's gotten beyond what he can endure. A lithe backless twirl in paisley starshine, you will die to him this day. In a moment. A moment of punishment and penance. Of dry aggregate and circles and dandelions and mayhem. You imitate something real, but we are not what we seem. He isn't very good at living, at breathing or kissing you, at walking down brick-clad alleyways in the dark. Isn't very good at bravery or love. Eyeliner heavy on lids, suit starched, your letter, in sweaty hands says "no," the paper wet from the rain, solemn and binding. He looks to the floor, looks beyond you to faux marble, slippery, running in all directions — PAST PRESENT FUTURE — gleaming in the fluorescent sunset slipped through dirty windows, double-glazed so no screams will be heard over the rain, drenching neon into the pavement.

He isn't very good in person.

He isn't what he seems.

(2014, May). Postcard Shorts

Water Cooler *Nu Allonge*

I loved her like a paper cut — my Jenny — all sunshine and red leather smirks, that girl of mine, bridled at the bottom of a ravine like a showroom mannequin doused in gasoline and the stench of roller-coaster fear and vomit. She was a white-hot hellcat, blessed top to bottom.

She sat in the cubicle next to mine — skin as pale and creamy as a manila envelope — and she sat there day after day decapitating political figures on her photo-editing program to pass the idle time between getting coffee and typing reports. She wore skirts: silk, and lace, and in the winter, black and red checked flannel with fringe at the slit. She was always fingering her garters when she thought no one was looking.

I was looking. I was always looking.

When she walked to the water cooler, she was like a floorshow at one of those Can-can clubs — swish and legs and perfumed panties. I imagined the warmth between her legs and how her lips would feel on mine. I imagined that she would like a dry martini if I made her one, and I imagined that she liked cats and colored lights and tinsel on her Christmas tree.

I wondered if she even noticed me at all, and often, I imagined that she did.

She never took a single sick day, so how could she not notice me and how I ached for her, how I wanted inside of her.

Her boss was a dick, always touching her with his fat fried-onion fingers while he rubbed his crotch into the back of her chair. It didn't make her feel sexy. It made her feel sad. She put binder clips on her fingers until her nails turned blue, and she scribbled her sadness down on the menus of all the local suicide buffets. That's how I got to know her — in the margins of a trashed menu where extra grease made everything more meaningful. She'd only ever smiled at me once, when I came around the corner near the fire exit and caught her ducking into the janitor's closet for a smoke. I started meeting her there, and we'd sit in the dark, in silence, listening to each other inhale and exhale as we gave up our dreams … seven minutes at a time.

(2012, February). Conotation Press An Online Artifact

Dramatic Effect

You wanted transcendence, wanted height, danger, the tracks blurred into murky distances behind and in front of you. You slipped, reached for it, starlight shining in your eyes, something you didn't have when I held your hand.

We didn't fold the laundry this morning, or straighten the tussled sheets. I picked up the mail, but you never opened it.

Yesterday you forgot to buy the raspberry tart I love so much, and I forgot the green tea with jasmine you drink from that old flowery teacup I broke last week and didn't tell you about.

How could I forget your eyes are blue, the concrete beneath you, dingy, muddled with oil.

I hold your hand now and wonder if you can hear me; was there ever a moment you could?

I suspect there was, but there's blood in your hair, and I'm sorry…

I'm sorry for everything: for you, for me, for us.

(2014, July). Fictionaut